PUFFIN BOOKS

Editor: Kaye Webb

A HUNDRED MILLION FRANCS

This is a tremendously exciting, highly original, and quite unpredictable story about a gang of Paris back-street children and a headless, battered wooden horse of a tricycle. It was their custom to take turns to ride it at top speed down the hill of the rue des Petits-Pauvres. Sometimes they crashed, sometimes not. Then strange things began to happen, and when a stranger offered them ten thousand francs for the horse, they were both impressed and suspicious. It disappeared, and the gang reported the matter to the police, but . . . a child's toy stolen? The police had more important things to spend their time on, and would not undertake to investigate this trivial crime. So the children tackled it themselves, and the scent led them into some fine exciting scenes in their wild country at the end of the Paris Metro line. The suspense and breathless interest makes this book line up with such classics as *Emil and the Detectives*, yet it has a light kind of echo too of the *William* books, and goes home to English readers as surely as it did to those French boys and girls who voted it the best book of its year in their country.

Richard Kennedy made the sketches for his illustrations in Paris, and has caught in them something of the authentic atmosphere of the scenes and characters.

For ages nine to twelve primarily, but also a joy to boys and girls much older.

A Hundred

Illustrated by Richard Kennedy

Million Francs

by PAUL BERNA

TRANSLATED FROM THE
FRENCH BY
John Buchanan-Brown

PENGUIN BOOKS
In association with The Bodley Head

Penguin Books Ltd, Harmondsworth, Middlesex, England
Penguin Books Australia Ltd, Ringwood, Victoria, Australia

—

First published in Paris as *Le Cheval sans tête* 1955
First published in Great Britain by The Bodley Head 1957
Published in Puffin Books 1960
Reprinted 1963, 1965, 1967, 1969, 1970, 1971

—

—

Made and printed in Great Britain
by Hazell Watson & Viney Ltd
Aylesbury, Bucks
Set in Linotype Granjon

Contents

CHAPTER I

Half Holiday

GABY and the rest of the gang were there in front of Fernand Douin's house at the top of the rue des Petits-Pauvres. One after another, the ten children mounted their horse and shot down the hill at top speed to the rue de la Vache Noire at the bottom. There the rider jumped to the ground and ran back up the slope dragging his steed behind him, to where his friends were impatiently waiting their turn.

Ever since Marion, the girl with the dogs, had knocked down old Monsieur Gédéon as he was crossing the rue

Cécile, they had posted little Bonbon at the cross-roads to hold up passers-by and to warn the gang if traffic were coming. The horse shot down the rue des Petits-Pauvres, making the most appalling noise from its three iron wheels. It was wonderful, and the cross-roads gave the ride a spice of danger that made it even more glorious. Then, right at the very end, the road made a steep climb, taking the horse and rider on to the bank round the Clos Pecqueux. As you breasted the rise you could see nothing but empty fields stretching grey to the horizon, so that for two seconds you felt as though you were flying. But if you failed to brake with your heels, in a flash you were over the crupper and flat on your back. When this happened the children called it a 'three-point landing'. At the end of each ride the horse toppled over on the kerb and its sides gave a hollow, mournful thump as they hit the hard cobblestones. No run was ever the same.

Fernand Douin had owned the horse for nearly a year. A rag-and-bone merchant from the Faubourg-Bacchus had exchanged it with Monsieur Douin for three packets of black tobacco, and Fernand had found it standing by his stocking on Christmas morning. For five whole minutes he had been too overcome with joy to utter a word. And yet to all outward appearance there was nothing very grand about the horse. It had never, even in the beginning, had a proper head, for although Monsieur Douin had stuck on a rough-and-ready cardboard affair, that hadn't lasted for more than two days. Marion had knocked it off on her first ride as she swept down at forty miles an hour into the back of Monsieur Mazurier's coal lorry. The head and the forelegs (the other casualties) were left behind in the gutter. Then the hind legs were snapped off short when the children rather rashly made a trial run through the tunnel on the Ponceau road. There is no need to tell you about the tail – there had never been one. All they now had left was the body, dapple grey under flaking varnish, with a little brown saddle painted on it. The rag-and-bone man had thrown in an old tricycle under-carriage – without either pedals or chain, it is true, but then you can't have everything. And there it was; a horse on three iron wheels that ran like a thoroughbred down the tarmac slope of the rue des Petits-Pauvres.

The children from Cité Ferrand were green with envy and said that this horse, a horse in the barest essentials, might just as well be a donkey or a pig (pig, they said, described it better than anything); and they asserted that the cowboys of the rue des Petits-Pauvres had no business to play the fool and risk their necks on an old pig with no head. For there was no denying that breaking the horse in had been a tough job. Fernand had lost most of one knee on the fence round César Aravant's scrap-yard; Marion had left a couple of teeth in the Ponceau tunnel, and it hadn't been very pleasant for either of them. But the knee got well in three days and second teeth had come through in a fortnight, and the horse still worked. And worked well, even by the standards of the smoky little back streets where nearly every man worked on the railways and kept the trains running.

After long negotiations it had eventually been agreed that the gang should use the horse once a day, so as to avoid putting too much strain upon it, each member getting two rides. No one had given the horse a long life. Even by reducing the running time like this, until Easter was the longest anyone had hoped for, but despite the most fearsome spills, it had held together, and still took you hell for leather down the rue des Petits-Pauvres. Gaby, the only one to cover the whole course without once putting on the 'brakes', had the record down to thirty-five seconds.

It was thanks to the horse that Fernand had been able to enrol his friend Marion in Gaby's gang, the closest of all the secret societies in Louvigny-Triage.

Being the only ones to take part in this daring sport had drawn the group even closer together. Gaby had purposely kept the numbers down and never accepted anyone over twelve, for, as he said, 'Once you're over twelve you become a complete fool and you're lucky if you don't stay like that for the rest of your life.' It was rather awkward, however, since Gaby himself was threatened by the age limit; but he secretly planned to raise it to fourteen and so benefit by this slight reprieve.

Now Tatave, little Bonbon's elder brother, was about to set off under the critical gaze of his friends.

'Look how heavy he is,' said Marion to Fernand. 'He shouldn't have more than one go, really. One of these days your horse will collapse under that great fat lump, and we'll see it coming up again with the wheels all squashed.'

A hundred yards below, little Bonbon, watching the junction of the rue Cécile, waved the all clear. Tatave shot past him like a rocket, head down, hands riveted to the rusty handle-bars of the horse.

'He's got the weight,' shrugged Juan, the little Spanish boy. 'But he'll never beat Gaby. He's a funk. Puts on the brakes fifty yards away from the rue de la Vache Noire. What we ought to do one day is to shove him off with his legs tied under the handle-bars.'

Farther on, the rue des Petits-Pauvres curved round out of sight of the watchers. They waited, but not for long. A great crash of breaking glass came up from the end of the road, then a wail, a flurry of curses, and the sharp crack of two good slaps.

'Crikey!' muttered Gaby, his jaw tightening, 'Tatave's had a smash!'

'Let's have a look,' suggested Fernand, who was rather worried about the horse.

'Zidore and Mélie stayed at the bottom,' said Marion; 'they'll get him out of any jam without our bothering.'

Gaby automatically glanced round. Apart from Marion, Fernand, and Juan, there was Berthe Gédéon, and Criquet Lariqué, the little darky from the Fauborg-Bacchus.

'We'll go as far as the rue Cécile,' he said, 'We can't leave them on their own; there may have been a real accident.'

When they got to the cross-roads they saw the others coming round the corner, their looks as gloomy as the dull December day. Zidore Loche was pulling the unfortunate horse along on two wheels, while beside him walked Tatave, limping slightly, rather red in the face and carrying the third wheel in his hand. Amélie Babin, the gang's first-aid expert, brought up the rear grinning from ear to ear and shaking with suppressed laughter. Every now and then she turned round to look down the rue des Petits-Pauvres, whence came strangled sounds of rage.

'It was bound to happen sooner or later!' cried Zidore as he came up. 'He always brakes at the wrong moment. Old Zigon was coming up from the main road with his hand-cart loaded with bottles just as Tatave comes round the bend. I stayed put, but what does Tatave do? Jams on his brakes and *smack!* Slap into the cart!'

Mélie rocked with laughter; her thin little face, framed by a black scarf over her fair hair, was split by a wicked grin.

'Tatave made a lovely three-point landing. You should have seen him! He went like a bomb right over the wire round the Clos. Honest! Old Zigon stood gaping like a cod-fish.'

'The old boy's O.K.!' asked Gaby.

'Yes, but a couple of dozen bottles got smashed and he's in an awful temper.'

'We'll bring him five dozen tomorrow evening,' said Marion. 'There's a whole stack of them in the pit behind the old trucks in the siding. No one else knows the place.'

Tatave had grazed his left knee badly and the seat of his trousers was plastered with thick yellow mud.

'Buckets and buckets and *buckets* of blood,' he muttered angrily.

Shamefacedly he handed the wheel to Fernand, while the others crowded round Zidore to examine the horse. Fifi, Marion's favourite dog, sniffed disdainfully at the cut and her dented wooden carcass.

'Well, this really looks as though we've had it now,' said Gaby, looking up in consternation. 'The front fork's snapped clean off; there are the two ends on the wheel. You've made a jolly good job of it, Tatave, I must say!'

Tatave blushed, hung his head, and sniffed.

The weight of the disaster silenced them all for a minute. Fernand's heart sank. His horse! There was nothing like it from Louvigny to Villeneuve-Saint-Georges. Marion slid her hand on to his shoulder.

'Your father will fix it for you,' she whispered. 'After all, it's not the first time it's happened.'

'I don't know,' Fernand replied, shaking his head; 'the fork's broken, and you know what that means; it's a really big job to repair it.'

Then little Bonbon came up from the rue Cécile, crying his eyes out.

'It's always the same!' he bellowed. 'I haven't had my second turn and you go and bust up the horse . . . '

Gaby turned to comfort the baby of the gang.

'Don't cry, Bonbon. Next time you shall have three goes instead of two.'

'My eye!' howled Bonbon, 'there won't be a next time. The horse is smashed to bits.'

Tatave, quite overwhelmed, tried to make himself as small as possible. Desperately he explained, 'When I saw old Zigon come up on the left I jammed on the brakes. Anyone would have done the same.'

'Oh yes!' retorted Gaby. 'You jammed on the brakes and went straight into him! You poor fool, the last thing you should have done was to put the brakes on.'

All the children giggled except Marion and Fernand, who picked up the wheel in one hand, the handle-bars in the other, and climbed slowly home, dragging the horse behind him. The others lagged behind, hands in pockets, discussing the accident.

But for the ten children and the occasional cat that slunk from door to door, the rue des Petits-Pauvres was deserted as the day drew in to its misty close. All the men were on the tracks, in the sidings, the signal boxes, or the railway workshops, and the women were either shopping in the Quartier-Neuf or were strolling round the Thursday Market, which went on until nightfall in front of the station.

Fernand carefully leant the horse against the garden wall and then went back to his friends.

'I'll leave it like that for the minute,' he said. 'Dad will see it when he comes in, and if he can mend the fork he'll get down to it at once.'

'What are we going to do now?' Zidore asked the others. 'It's hardly four.'

'We could take a look round the market,' suggested Gaby. 'And I could do with a bite to eat!'

They all turned to Marion, who was treasurer to the gang. She felt in the pockets of her coat. It was a man's jacket cut down to fit her, and under it she wore a short grey skirt which looked like a dancer's *tutu*, from which her long skinny legs protruded like two sticks.

'We've just enough to buy a round of *polonais*,' she said, counting the money again. 'And then only if Madame Macherel doesn't ask for the twenty francs from last time.'

'Well, the only thing then is to send someone else,' suggested Gaby. 'She doesn't know the darky; he's never round there. Off you go, Criquet – you'll find us down by the station.'

Madame Macherel's bakery, among its other cakes, made a rather horrible sort of sticky black pudding at ten francs the slice. This was the celebrated *polonais*. It was dear but it was sweet, and it dropped into your stomach like lead and kept you quiet until the next meal.

Slowly Gaby's gang crossed the Square de la Libération, a piece of brownish turf surrounded by spindly trees. Gaby took the lead with Zidore and Juan. Then came Tatave, Fernand, and little Bonbon, the latter kicking his toes in anger as, for the fourth time, he heard his elder brother recount the disastrous results of putting on the brakes. The three girls brought up the rear, skipping from one foot to the other in spite of the bitter cold and the disappointments of the afternoon.

Fifi trotted from one group to the other in search of a pat or a friendly word. He was a short-haired yellowish dog, with a whippet's body and a long thin tail like a rat's. Marion had found him, as she found all her dogs, below the allotments beyond Louvigny-Cambrouse, as they called it in Louvigny-Triage. Behind the fields were some old ponds, all overgrown with a sort of jungle of bushes, where people from the neighbourhood, and even from Paris, used to leave their sick, injured, and dying dogs. Marion befriended them, undaunted by their diseases or wounds, cared for them, put them on their feet again as though by magic, and then found homes for them with the rail-men in the old town. But she never let them go until she had trained them to obey her, and her charges never forgot the special note of Marion's whistle. So it was that at least half the dogs in the neighbourhood had passed through her hands, and she had only to walk across the Faubourg-Bacchus for a whole pack of wretched mongrels to run at her heels nearly wagging their tails off with the joy of seeing her. She had never less than a dozen on her hands, feeding them on stale bread and scraps that the shop-keepers round about were only too pleased to give her. This knock-kneed, mangy pack was kennelled at the bottom of the garden in a collection of old wooden boxes that looked rather like a lot of rabbit-hutches. Marion's mother, Madame Fabert, had many a time shaken her head and raised a despairing eye to heaven, but she had never dared to do anything to discourage her daughter.

The gang had reached the corner of the square when Gaby turned with a wink and called to them, 'Roublot's there, I can hear him from here.'

They hurried on. The little Thursday Market ran all round the edges of the square and even pushed itself into the roadway of the rue des Alliés and on to the station approaches. It was a foggy evening and many of the market people had lit the acetylene flares on their stalls, throwing a fairground glare of white and golden light on the crowd. The powerful whistle of the engines shunting in the nearby sidings sounded all the time in the background, and every now and then the whole town seemed to tremble as an express thundered through the station at sixty miles an hour.

The children slipped into the crowd. As usual, Roublot had put up his stall in the far corner of the square under the rosy glow of the lights of the Café Parisien. He brought out all his patter to draw the customers, but no one seemed to be very interested in his vegetable-graters. He was a nasty-looking specimen, with a heavy, sallow face that mirrored his petty dishonesty. One day the summer before he had accused Gaby of pocketing a gas-lighter, and Gaby had been hauled up before Inspector Sinet, which was a serious matter. Gaby hadn't stolen a single thing, he wasn't the sort who would, and he never had a thief in his gang either. In the end Gaby's father, Monsieur Joye, a mechanic at the railway workshops who weighed a good seventeen stone, had cleared the business by going down the next Thursday and telling Roublot, in front of everyone, that if there was any more nonsense he'd give Roublot something to remember him by. That had been quite enough, and from then on, whenever Roublot set up his pitch at Louvigny, Gaby got his revenge by bringing the gang to cock a snook at him. In any case it was fun to hear his cheap-jack patter and there was something raffish about him that attracted the older ones.

All at once Roublot saw the children coming up to his rickety stall.

'Ah, here comes my young audience at last!' he cried, putting on a good-natured voice. 'They're the real experts. They never buy anything, but they appreciate the marvels of modern science which are at the housewife's service. Gather round, children – back a bit there – while I give you a demonstration of the Fransfix Mincer. Here it is, the one and only genuine multi-purpose mincer on the market! Here's the machine to squeeze your lemons, grate your cheese, slice your vegetables, or mince your beef. The secret's in the way you use it, and the makers have sent me to Louvigny just to put this marvel of precision in your hands. Look, I take this carrot for a start . . .'

Little Bonbon and Berthe Gédéon stood on tiptoe to see the carrot go into the machine.

'He won't sell one,' whispered Marion. 'Those old things only work once: next day they're in the dustbin.'

'He never does sell anything,' added Gaby, 'or very little. Anyway, he couldn't care less. You'd think he was here for some other purpose."

Fernand turned towards Gaby in surprise. 'What else?' he asked.

'I don't know,' Gaby answered with a grin. 'A lot of people make a show of selling a thing when they're up to some dodge on the quiet.'

Just then Criquet arrived, quite out of breath, but carrying ten pieces of *polonais* carefully wrapped up in greaseproof paper. They all pushed round him as Gaby shared the parcel out, giving the two biggest pieces to Bonbon and Criquet (because he had bought the *polonais*), while Tatave got the smallest to teach him not to go and break up the horse again. Then, jaws munching steadily, they turned to watch Roublot's flying fingers feed a raw carrot, a potato, an apple, an orange, and a bit of cheese into one end of the mincer, to produce a most revolting mixture at the other.

Gaby swallowed the last mouthful, licked his fingers, and leaned against Fernand. 'Look,' he whispered.

Fernand nodded. He saw. Marion, meanwhile, bent down to give Fifi a bit of her *polonais*, and as she got up she, too, saw what had drawn the attention of the boys.

Roublot continued to demonstrate his mincers, a stream of nonsense pouring from his lips, his hands dismantling his machine with his usual speed and skill, but with his mind obviously on something else. His face was slightly turned to his right, towards the grimy station buildings, and, all the time he kept up his flow of patter, his little black eyes were gazing with passionate intensity in that direction.

Gaby slowly slipped behind Tatave and moved away unconcernedly. There was quite a crowd milling round the two market stalls in this corner of the square, which made it hard to see at first glance what was putting Roublot on the watch. All at once his eyes fell upon the pavement behind the stalls, reflecting here and there the light from them. A thin stream of people passed along on their way home from the Depot, workers going to their lodgings in Cité Ferrand, Arab dockers from Petit-Louvigny, and among them a tall, thin figure in a battered hat and a bottle-green trench coat: Inspector Sinet.

Gaby could watch the slow progress of the trench coat,

disappearing and reappearing at regular intervals between the stalls. Then he thought that the Inspector hurried a little, as though he were keeping up with someone else. Gaby's eyesight was excellent, and at last he picked up the outline of the other man among the passers-by who strolled along the pavement, singly, or in small groups. He was a burly figure in a blue boiler-suit and night or day you could see hundreds like him in the streets of Louvigny-Triage. One behind the other the two men left the crowd and were swallowed up in the dusk of the Square de la Libération. Gaby saw no more.

He turned back to Roublot, who still held his audience with a flood of patter. A housewife from Louvigny-Cambrouse and five factory girls from Cité Ferrand had joined the gang. The cheap-jack stood with his hat pushed slightly back, the sweat gleaming on his forehead. Marion hadn't seen Sinet, still less the man in the blue boiler-suit who had been prowling round the market, but her keen eyes missed nothing else.

'Roublot's scared,' she muttered.

You notice things like that by accident and don't attach a great deal of importance to them: two minutes later you forget all about them and it's sometimes a long time before you find the true meaning behind them.

Roublot minced away the whole time with a fury of speed that had the air of panic.

'That old mincer isn't worth a bean,' declared little Bonbon suddenly and loudly, with devastating conviction.

This made everyone laugh and broke the spell. The audience melted away and the housewife was left facing a furious Roublot. Gaby led his gang towards the haberdashers' stalls at the other end of the market, on the town side.

Half-way there Fernand turned automatically towards the rosy lights of the Café Parisien.

'What are you looking at?' Marion asked him.

'Roublot's gone!' was the astonished answer. 'He's left everything, and vanished before you could say knife.'

As they came to the corner of the rue des Alliés, Bonbon and Tatave's mother, Madame Louvrier, came out of the crowd, clutching two great baskets of vegetables, and called the children to her. Regretfully they left the gang.

'Don't worry about the horse!' Fernand called to Tatave.

It was getting late. The night was falling fast, throwing mournful shadows over the street and the smoking railway lines in the background. Their half holiday was over.

Soon Criquet Lariqué and Juan slipped off towards the Faubourg-Bacchus; Berthe Gédéon said good-bye to the others and hurried away to Cité Ferrand, and then it was Gaby's turn to leave with Zidore and Mélie. All three lived some distance away, at the junction of the main road and the rue Aubertin. Marion and Fernand were left alone.

The boy looked up at the clock of the old church of Louvigny, whose pointed steeple stuck up at the end of the square and overhung the rue des Petits-Pauvres.

'Dad should be home by now,' he murmured.

Marion whistled her dog. Hand in hand they made their way to the rue des Petits-Pauvres, cutting across the square. Suddenly, as they turned the corner, Fernand saw something lying right across the pavement in front of his house. He approached wide-eyed; it was his horse.

'You ought to have taken it inside,' said Marion.

Carefully Fernand picked up his unfortunate horse and stood it on its back wheels.

'Someone must have knocked it down as they went by,'

he said angrily. 'How stupid of them. I put it up against the wall so that it shouldn't get in the way.'

'There're some people who knock things down just for fun,' said Marion. 'Look and see that nothing's broken.'

Fernand turned the wheels and felt the body. All was well.

'It's O.K.,' he said in relief. 'If Dad can mend the fork, we'll be able to start again on Saturday or Sunday. Dad won't let us down, you know that.'

Lifting his head, he was suddenly aware of a shadowy form furtively emerging from the square. By the yellow light of the street lamp Fernand saw that it was Roublot. The cheap-jack had his hat pulled down over his eyes, and his overcoat, which was unbuttoned, swirled around him. He pulled up short and seemed quite put out to see the children.

'What do you want?' asked Fernand, in unconcealed hostility. 'This is our place.'

Roublot didn't answer. Instead, he came on with his arms out-stretched, as though to pin the children against the wall. As soon as Marion saw this, she raised two fingers to her lips and let out a piercing whistle that re-echoed through the empty street.

To his horror, Roublot saw three enormous dogs appear as if by magic from the gloom at the end of the street. They were great hairy brutes, hideously ugly, and they loped along without a sound. It was almost unbelievable how silently and rapidly those dogs arrived. Roublot half turned, and made for the square as fast as his legs would carry him. Marion burst out laughing. The three dogs sped past her: César, a Great Dane, Hugo, a boar-hound, and Fritz, an Alsatian – three of the fiercest dogs in the district, and all former patients in the dogs' hospital of the rue des Petits-Pauvres. Marion clacked her tongue against the roof of her mouth. At once they ended their chase and came to heel like well-trained dogs, tails wagging hard against their flanks. Fernand was weak with laughter.

'That's nothing,' Marion told him. 'If I whistle as I cross the Faubourg-Bacchus, in a couple of seconds I've got five dozen of them at my heels. Dogs never forget.'

She patted the three hounds. They made friends with Fifi, cocked a leg against the wall of Monsieur Douin's house, and then without more ado went about their business, disappearing down the rue Cécile.

'Would you like me to stay a little longer with you?' Marion asked. 'Mum's expecting me back, but five minutes won't make any odds.'

'It's not worth it,' answered Fernand, looking towards the station. 'Dad won't be long now.'

'But if Roublot comes back?'

'He won't, the great coward.'

'I'd like to know what he's after,' muttered Marion, with a hint of anxiety in her voice.

'Some people are like that,' said Fernand. 'They go for you for nothing. Roublot couldn't take little Bonbon's joke, I expect. Anyway, you'd better be getting on, Marion; you don't want to be late.'

Marion said good-bye and made off down the hill with Fifi running in front of her. When she got to the corner of the rue Cécile, she turned and gave a last wave, and that, for Fernand, was the end of their half holiday.

When Monsieur Douin came home from work he found his son crouched in the doorway, one arm round the horse.

'Mum's getting a meal for some people in the Quartier-Neuf,' Fernand told his father. 'She won't be in till eight.'

'You should have waited for me with a neighbour,

instead of standing about in the cold,' his father scolded. 'Come on, in you go.'

Fernand led the way indoors, dragging the horse behind on its two wheels.

'What have you been up to this afternoon?' asked Monsieur Douin.

'The . . . the horse got broken,' stammered his son with lowered head. 'The front wheel came off.'

'What, again?' sighed Monsieur Douin, good-humouredly.

'This time I'm afraid its serious.'

Monsieur Douin turned the light on in the kitchen and put down his haversack on the table. He was a quiet, kindly man, with a long, greying moustache and an air almost of sadness.

'Well, let's have a look at it, then,' he said, lowering himself into a chair.

His son pushed the horse backwards into the kitchen. The two remaining wheels were never oiled, and they screeched dreadfully as they turned. Monsieur Douin took hold of the handle-bars and leaned forward to see what the damage was.

'Good heavens!' he said with a start. 'The fork's smashed.'

Fernand shrugged despairingly. Monsieur Douin sighed again, and then, balancing the handle-bars across his knee, he examined the broken fork more closely, running a mechanic's experienced hand over the metal-work.

'Well,' he said at last. 'I can't do anything with it. Ordinary solder won't hold it. If I did that, then you really would break your necks.'

Fernand was in despair. He began to cry quietly. The tears streamed down his cheeks and splashed on the linoleum floor. His father saw him out of the corner of his eye. Even more gently he balanced the handle-bars on the edge of the table.

'Cheer up, old fellow,' he said in his husky voice. 'Listen, tomorrow morning I'll go down to the car factory on my way to work. Monsieur Rossi in the workshops will forge a new fork for us in his spare time. That sort of thing's nothing to him. It's a nuisance we can't take the old one off. You'd have to saw it through just there.' Then he chuckled. 'All my mates are going to pull my leg, though, when they see me roll up with this old nag under my arm!'

'Well, you could take the two wheels off,' suggested Fernand, smiling through his tears. 'That would give you less to carry. The horse hasn't got a head and without the wheels he won't look like anything, so people won't laugh at you.'

Monsieur Douin got his tool-box out, and soon the two of them were hard at work on the horse. Madame Douin laughed when, coming in at about half past eight, she found father and son on the floor beside the horse.

'I know,' she murmured; 'Zidore's mother told me all about it on my way home. So Tatave saw stars, did he! One of these days, I warn you, you'll go and break your neck.'

'Let him be,' answered Monsieur Douin. 'Let the kids enjoy themselves. If they don't have their fun now they never will. Once they're twelve it's too late.'

Fernand got up to help his mother. Monsieur Douin took the two wheels off and pushed the carcass into the hall. Then he washed his hands carefully under the tap. His wife looked up as she heard him whistle.

'You enjoyed yourself just the same thirty years ago in the old barn in the Faubourg-Bacchus, didn't you?' she asked him laughing.

CHAPTER 2

Good-bye to the Horse

MARION and her mother lived at the end of the rue des Petits-Pauvres in a tumbledown house on the corner fronting the rue de la Vache Noire. No one had ever been able to say for certain how this country lane of a street had got its name. Marion held to the opinion, and having it under her nose the whole time she could hardly do otherwise, that the Black Cow was none other than the old engine which had been left to rust in the middle of the Clos Pecqueux for the last thirty years. Once there had been a siding there, but the rails had gradually been taken away until all that were left were those that ran, half-buried in the soil, under this museum piece. Reddish-brown in the summer sun and as unexpected as a hippopotamus in a field of daisies, the Black Cow only really became black in the rain, when its mournful shape was threateningly outlined against the watery sky-line. At night, when the autumn and winter storms were raging, the west wind would howl through its rust-pitted old boiler and draw frenzied answers from Marion's twelve dog-patients.

The next evening, after school, Gaby took the strongest members of the gang with him to the no man's land where César Aravant's yard lay. It was a regular scrap-heap, with dismantled wooden trucks, piles of rusty iron-work, half-burnt sleepers, and twisted rails. Marion knew just where to go and she led her friends to the empty bottles hidden in a trench alongside the endmost truck.

They were piled three deep; the earth on top of them and the grass all round them had practically cemented them together.

They made a chain and in next to no time had filled the pram lent by Berthe Gédéon with forty or fifty bottles. Then Gaby set off for the Faubourg-Bacchus with Zidore and Fernand, each taking it in turn to push the pram. Tatave still limped from his accident, and so dodged the work and went with the girls.

Old Zigon could hardly believe his eyes when the three children brought their load into his wooden hut. His stock consisted solely of the bottles of wine he had drained himself. He hadn't done too badly, by all appearances.

As they came back by way of the station, Gaby remarked with a touch of melancholy, 'The horse wasn't much, just an old wooden body on three wheels, but you do miss it. Ever since yesterday I've felt as though there was nothing to do. Do you think your father will keep his word, Fernand?'

'Anyway, he did take the horse with him this morning,' Fernand answered. 'Monsieur Rossi is sure to have a shot at it; he has all the tools for the job. All we can do is wait – but don't count too much on having it back by Sunday.'

'What can we do?' groaned Zidore.

'There's a cowboy film on at the "Eden",' said Fernand, 'Marion saw the photos on the way to school. It's in technicolor and she says it looks smashing.'

'A trip to the flicks costs too much,' sighed Gaby. 'Juan and the darky can never pay – I know it's not their fault, but someone has to fork out for them. Anyway, we're broke.'

'Marion'll take care of that,' Fernand replied.

The Café Parisien was full. As they passed, Gaby glanced through the windows.

'You don't often see Roublot around, except for market day on Thursday,' he suddenly remarked to his friends. 'Here, take a look.'

The cheap-jack was sitting at the end of the room opposite a couple of toughs in fur-lined lumber-jackets. They were deep in conversation, leaning across the table, their hats nearly touching. Whatever they were talking about seemed to be very important.

Fernand glanced over his shoulder as he heard someone hurrying up behind him. The light from the café fell on Inspector Sinet's bottle-green trench coat. Zidore and Gaby nudged each other. Across the Inspector's right cheek was a pink strip of sticking-plaster which contrasted oddly with his muddy complexion. He didn't notice the children and paid as little attention to the customers in the café. He was soon swallowed up in the darkness.

'He's got a lovely black eye,' laughed Gaby, 'and a fresh one at that!'

'But he seemed awfully pleased with himself,' added Zidore in surprise.

'Remember last night?' Gaby went on. 'He was following a bloke from the station to the Square de la Libération. Something must have happened over there. . . . I wonder what it was.'

Monsieur Douin came home at eight, empty-handed. Fernand didn't expect anything, but he stood wide-eyed watching his father without daring to utter a word. The latter shook his head:

'I didn't have time to see Monsieur Rossi before I left,' he apologized. 'Anyway, he's doing the job for nothing so I can hardly ask him to hurry it up.'

All Saturday the rain poured down. After school Fernand left his friends and went straight home, for the weather was too bad for them to do anything interesting. Marion was not with him. She was still out trying to get together the money for the gang's Sunday visit to the cinema. They had all emptied their pockets and she had got half the amount that way. She promised herself that she would find the rest before dark. But no one believed in miracles and they all thought that the cinema would go the same way as the horse.

'Why don't we sell the bottles?' Tatave had suggested. 'Old Zigon would be awfully glad to take the lot.'

'There are some things you can't sell,' was Marion's stern answer. 'Those bottles are anyone's property. Just because I've found them it doesn't mean I can do what I like with them. And what would it look like if we did sell the bottles to the old man? We may be broke but we're not a bunch of spivs.'

As the clock struck six she reached Fernand's house. He was looking after the house, his mother was out, and he was bored to tears.

'I've got the money,' she said with a smile, 'and a little bit extra too. I hope that'll satisfy the others. The pictures aren't a patch on the horse, though.'

'How did you manage it?' asked Fernand.

'Oh, an old lady in the Quartier-Neuf made up the money for me. The vet in Louvigny-Cambrouse had poisoned her peke with a whole lot of medicines. I cured it in a couple of days. I won't generally take any money for curing dogs, but this time I made an exception because of the horse. We can't spend Sunday twiddling our thumbs, can we?'

She had only been there five minutes, when they heard

the key turn in the lock. Monsieur Douin swung the door open.

'I've got it,' he said, with a wink. 'Give me a hand to get it inside.'

The rain had stopped and the roadway gleamed under the yellow glow of the street lamps. The rue des Petits-Pauvres was at its liveliest on a Saturday night. Lights shone out from the open doorways, groups of railwaymen came home from the station, and the little bar, 'L'Auvergnat', on the corner of the rue des Alliés, never emptied before ten o'clock.

The headless horse stood on its three wheels on the concrete path through the front garden, an old coal-sack thrown over its battered body.

'Monsieur Rossi put back the wheels himself,' said Monsieur Douin. 'He greased the hubs and straightened the bent spokes. He's done a good job. Don't forget to thank him.'

All three wheeled the horse into the kitchen to admire it under the light. Fernand pulled the sack away and ran the tips of his fingers over the new fork. Monsieur Rossi had given it a coat of green paint.

'That's more like it,' cried Monsieur Douin. 'That's good and firm.'

Marion grabbed a rag and wiped the dust off the body while Fernand tested each wheel in turn to see that they ran true. Monsieur Douin watched them, nervously rubbing his hands together.

'A funny thing happened on my way home,' he began. 'A chap came out of the Café Parisien, and without a by-your-leave he takes me by the arm and asks me what I've got. I pull back the sacking and show him the horse. "Right," he says; "I'll give you five thousand francs for it." I thought he was joking; but oh, no, he followed me as far as the square, raising his price the whole time. When I reached the corner he was offering ten. I had a job to get rid of him, I can tell you.'

The two children looked up.

'It wasn't Roublot, was it?' asked Fernand.

'No, I don't know who it was. Big chap, not too badly dressed, in spite of a two-day growth on his chin. He didn't seem to be pulling my leg either. All the same, ten thousand for that old thing – why, it's crazy!'

Marion and Fernand, rather worried, looked at each other without a word. All the pleasure the surprise had given them vanished in a flash. The horse was back, but Monsieur Douin's story had spoiled it all. The latter noticed his son's worried expression and, misunderstanding it, growled:

'I suppose I shouldn't have told you that. Now I've given you ideas. Just you get it firmly in your head, my lad, that that horse is worth nothing! Just nothing!'

'It's my horse,' Fernand answered angrily, 'and I wouldn't sell it for twice the money – and your friend can put that in his pipe!'

*

Of course it was Fernand who made the first run to test the new fork.

'She won't snap in a hurry,' he said as he climbed the hill again. 'The horse has never run better.'

The dry weather had returned and now and then the sun would break through the overcast sky. In no time they had arranged the order in which they would take their turns and the afternoon's sport began merrily. Gaby, in spite of his Sunday best, took some hair-raising risks and managed to break his own record twice running. Little Bonbon had his three goes. The girls, their hair flying wildly in the wind, shot down the slope. Angry or laughing faces peered out of the windows all along the rue des Petits-Pauvres. Passers-by jumped on to the narrow pavement as the horse thundered by, only just missing them, and shouted curses or encouragement at the rider.

'Come on!' shrieked the children all down the route.

And on came Tatave, his left knee bandaged, his heel bouncing on the tarmac as he tried to slow his mount; on came Marion, grinning broadly. Her black scarf flying out behind her wiped the nose of an old grey horse that was drawing an ice-cart across the junction of the rue Cécile. The carter stood up in his seat waving his whip and shouting at her. When it reached the short slope at the end, the horse without a head seemed to buck, all three wheels came off the ground, and the rider was ungently deposited on the muddy bank by the roadside.

As it got later, people taking their Sunday afternoon stroll filled the rue des Petits-Pauvres, returning from the café, the cinema, or the football ground in Louvigny-Cambrouse. Fernand was first to spot the strangers, two burly individuals whose dress marked them out among the local people. They had already walked up and down the left-hand pavement as far as the rue de la Vache Noire several times, without seeming to be interested in the thunderous cavalry charges. They were both laughing and talking away, and no one had taken much notice of these two passers-by, unremarkable except for the fine fur-lined lumber-jackets they were wearing. As he was coming to the end of his last run, Fernand saw that they had taken their stand on the right-hand pavement in front of Marion's gate. Half the gang were at the bottom to cheer each rider as he came down, and the two men stood motionless, watching the scene, scowling and never saying a word.

'That's all for tonight,' said Fernand as he jumped to the ground.

Marion too had seen the men, and she nodded a warning to the bigger ones while Gaby silenced their protests. Surrounding Fernand in a compact body, the ten children climbed back up the hill with the horse. With the help of Marion and Gaby, he put it in the kitchen. Monsieur Douin, stretched out in carpet slippers in front of the fire, watched them good humouredly.

'Well, how did it go?' he asked Fernand.

'It couldn't have been better if it was new,' was the answer.

Then, after a moment's silence:

'What is a nuisance is that certain people hung round for quite a time. I don't like it . . .'

Monsieur Douin took his pipe out of his mouth. 'What people?'

'Here, have a look,' said Fernand, gently inching the door open.

Monsieur Douin peered through the crack. It was getting dark, and the rue des Petits-Pauvres had emptied in the meanwhile. There was a coming and going about the little bar on the corner, but the rest of the street had returned to its usual quiet. The two men in lumber-jackets had come slowly up the hill on the opposite pavement. They passed the house without turning their heads. Softly Monsieur Douin closed the door.

'Ten thousand francs for a horse with no head,' he grumbled as he settled himself into his chair once more. 'I'll be darned if it isn't that same pair. Well, some folk do get a bee in their bonnets!'

'It was the same man as last night?' asked Fernand.

'I don't know: he could be the taller of the two, but I can't be positive. It was getting too dark to see properly. In any case, if anyone upsets you, just you tell me. Gaby, you tell your father, do you hear?'

'Just let them try,' laughed Marion.

*

The strangers waited until the following Tuesday to make contact with the gang. It was nearly five. There was a clear patch in the sky in the west and the setting sun stained the clouds with crimson and tinged with pink the houses in the rue des Petits-Pauvres.

Half the gang was with Gaby in front of Fernand's house, while the others were waiting at the rue de la Vache Noire, shrieking with excitement every time the horse came shooting round the bend. Little Bonbon was, as usual, on point duty at the corner of the rue Cécile. Zidore had just taken his second turn and they had watched him thunder over the cross-roads at top speed, yelling like a stuck pig. Three minutes passed, but the road remained empty; there was no sign of Zidore coming back.

'What's he up to now?' growled Juan, who was impatiently waiting his turn.

All had been quiet for two days, and Gaby had not given another thought to Monsieur Douin's story. Suddenly he gave a start.

'Come on!' he called to the others. 'Quick!'

They ran down to the end of the road. Fernand, Zidore, and the three girls were having a bitter argument with the two men in lumber-jackets. One of them had grabbed the handle-bars of the horse and was trying to jerk it out of the children's grasp, but Berthe and Marion held on to the left wheel and Zidore and Fernand to the

right, while Mélie gripped the stumps of the back legs. All five were shouting at the tops of their voices to the accompaniment of Marion's twelve dogs, who were jumping up and down against the fence round her garden, barking their heads off. When the reinforcements came up the man let go.

'They want to buy our horse,' Fernand called to Gaby, 'but we won't sell. . . .'

'Come on – ten thousand francs, then,' cried the taller of the two men. 'That's not something to turn up your nose at: why, you could get a new horse for that with pedals, head, and all.'

'Nuts' retorted Gaby. 'They haven't made those for years. Anyway, this is Fernand's horse; it's all we've got to play with, and *it isn't for sale*.'

'Hear that, Pépé?' laughed the man as he turned to his companion. 'They're a close lot round here.'

Slowly the other unbuttoned his lumber-jacket and took out a fat wallet.

'Cut it out!' he threatened. 'Here's the money – take it and clear out. We want that horse.'

'You shan't have it!' was Gaby's resolute reply.

Fernand had quietly pushed the horse up against the fence, and the ten children drew themselves up along the pavement to defend it. The sunset flamed in their faces and threw up the dark, thick-set figures of the two strangers where they stood opposite them in front of the grassy bank. In the background in the Clos Pecqueux the rusty shape of the Black Cow looked down on this strange scene.

'We'll see about that,' growled the one called Pépé, as he made towards Gaby.

But Gaby stood firm, and the others closed up on either side of him.

Marion laughed to herself. She was already bringing two fingers to her lips.

Pépé's piggy little eyes gleamed. 'Wait till the toe of my boot gets you, my lad,' he muttered between his teeth.

'I bet it doesn't,' snorted Gaby. 'My Dad's the only one who can lay a finger on me, and he has to catch me first.'

The children burst out laughing.

'Come on, Ugly,' said Pépé, turning to his companion, 'let's start with this one ...'

Marion gave a whistle. As Pépé jumped at him, Gaby dropped on one knee and caught him a blow in the pit of the stomach which he didn't like very much. The crook staggered back, winded, and sat down hard in the gutter. In his turn Ugly attacked Gaby and caught him in a bear-hug. In was at that instant that the first dog bounded up.

It was Hugo the boar-hound. Soundlessly he sped along the rue de la Vache Noire in the shadow of the bank. He caught Ugly square on the shoulders and made him scream with fear as he twisted and turned to avoid his jaws. Pépé struggled to his feet only to find himself face to face with Fritz and César, who came round the corner at full speed, the Great Dane's jaws gaping wide.

The three dogs, with lolling tongues and eyes glowing like hot coals, hurled themselves on the toughs and began to tear the lumber-jackets, which gave them wonderful toothholds, from off their backs. The cloth ripped away and they fell on the padding and the coney-fur lining. It was fascinating to watch them. The two men rolled on the ground protecting their faces with their arms, and kicking out to save their shins and ankles, while Marion's twelve patients barked a tally-ho from behind the railings.

'Help! help!' screamed Ugly.

Marion was only waiting for that to call off her hounds. Obediently they came to heel behind her. Hugo was still

holding a fur collar between his teeth, while a torn sleeve hung from César's jaws. Fritz licked his chops. He was the most dangerous of the three, a crafty cut-throat who would wait for hours behind a wall just for the fun of leaping out on a solitary passer-by. Breathing heavily, the two men got up.

'Well,' said Gaby in his most polite voice, 'it really was nice to hear you bellow for help. Now get out and stay out!'

'My dogs never bark,' added Marion, 'so watch out that they don't get you before you know what's happening. As for the horse – take a good look at it and say good-bye to it.'

Half running, half limping the two roughs went down the rue de la Vache Noire to where it joined the main road.

'They won't come back again,' muttered Zidore as he watched them go. 'In another minute those dogs would have torn them to bits.'

'If they've got something at the back of their minds they're bound to come back,' said Juan knowingly.

Fernand was intrigued by the Spaniard's remark.

'Well, what's so wonderful about my horse?' he exclaimed. 'It's not solid gold; it's a wreck!'

'You never know,' Juan replied. 'Perhaps there's something special about it that we don't know but they do.'

They examined the horse with new interest, as though they had only just got it. But the horse was still the same, and all the trouble they had had with it hadn't made it grow a new head. Its only value was to give endless pleasure to the ten children who took it out every day. Criquet Lariqué stroked the battered old body with his little black hands.

'Well, I can't understand it,' declared Gaby with a

shake of the head. 'If the kids from Cité Ferrand or the Faubourg Bacchus had been after it, it would have made sense – but two big blokes like that!'

The sun was going down quickly. Darkness was covering the town like a flood, drowning the slums of Louvigny-Cambrouse, the sidings, the factories, and the smoky railway tracks where the coloured signal lights sprang up as though by magic and stretched away into the distance. All of a sudden it got colder.

'Let's go,' said Marion, shivering under her coat.

Without a word they moved off up the rue des Petits-Pauvres, all ten of them closing round the horse, which Fernand was pulling along by the handle-bars. Instinctively each one had a hand on the hollow old body – it was their horse.

True to his promise, that same evening Fernand told his father the whole story, leaving nothing out. Monsieur Douin didn't say a word; the whole thing seemed to have quite overcome him. After a moment's thought he turned round to look at the horse stabled at the end of the kitchen. The shadows gave it an air of mystery.

At last he murmured, 'I wonder if it wouldn't be better to tell the police about it.'

But he didn't. The rumour ran that Inspector Sinet had made an important arrest, a thing which happened once in a blue moon in this law-abiding neighbourhood. You could hardly go to him with some story of a children's horse after that. In any case it would only make things unpleasant if he was brought in. Sinet was always chasing the children and summoning their parents to the station. It made him feel important, though it didn't make him very popular in the neighbourhood. The answer to Monsieur Douin's question was no.

None the less, Monsieur Douin was worried, and on his

way home the following evening he went as far as the sinister-looking allotments near the Faubourg-Bacchus where the rag-and-bone men made their home.

By the light of an oil lamp old Blache was picking over some clothes at one end of his hut. Winter and summer the old fellow wore a pair of ragged overcoats sewn together, and a broad-brimmed hat like a priest's, green with age, jammed down to his ears. He had an odd red-and-black shaggy beard which he trimmed with a pair of blunt scissors once a fortnight. Although you might be put off by the fact that he was filthy dirty, he was a good enough fellow at heart and a great talker. He was pleased to see Monsieur Douin and at once drew a great bottle of red wine out of the cupboard. The two men sat down to the table near the lamp.

'Well,' said Monsieur Douin, scratching his head nervously, 'I've come to see you about this darned horse.'

'The horse!' said Blache quite flabbergasted.

'Yes, the horse on wheels.'

The rag-and-bone man flung himself back in his chair with a roar of laughter.

'I didn't quite follow you,' he said. 'You see, for the last two days I've been thinking over buying a real horse from the clod-hoppers in Louvigny!'

Monsieur Douin told old Blache only a part of the gang's troubles as he brought the conversation round to the one question he felt was worth answering – where had the horse come from?

'Now you ask me,' answered the rag-and-bone man, 'I remember I came across it in an odd way. But don't get thinking it's got anything to do with what's happened to your boy. You know Zigon, the bottle merchant? About this time last year he tipped me that they were clearing the bomb damage in Petit-Louvigny at last. You know they copped it when they were going for the railways in '44. Anyway, they'd got a stack of junk that the demolition men didn't want and anyone could go along and help themselves so long as they kept their eyes open and didn't fall down and break their necks in the cellars that had been left opened up. I took my handcart and off I went. But I was too late, my mates had taken all that was worth having, there wasn't a rag or a bit of old iron left. But I had a good look round, and what do you think I found? A little animal's head under a heap of plaster, looking up at me with its round eyes. First I thought it was a dog that had got caught digging around! I got out my crowbar and shifted the stuff away a bit when out it rolled, and there at my feet was a wooden horse's head! It was cut clean through. I think a bomb splinter must have taken the head straight off. So I had a good look round, and I found the rest of the animal. You won't believe me, but it gave me quite a turn. "If I go on looking," I said to myself, "I'll find the kid who was on it." I'd nearly cleared the wheels when a couple of fellows came along the path through the ruins, hands in pockets. Nasty customers they were, shifty-eyed, real fox-faced both of them. "Don't get up!" said the bigger of the two. "Make yourself at home. Leave the key under the mat when you go!"

'That type doesn't impress me very much, so I told him, quite politely, to go and lose himself.

' "I know it sounds a bit odd to you," he said, quite calmly, "but this horse used to be mine when the house was still standing."

'What would you have done if you'd been in my shoes, Douin? Straight out I said, "Well, take the horse, then." That made him laugh.

' "Not worth it," he answered. "It's not much use to me: I go a darned sight faster on four wheels now."

'Then I said to him, after I'd had a good look at him, "I knew all the kids in Petit-Louvigny," I said, "so I ought to know you; who are you?"

'He didn't like that, no more did his mate.

' "Mind your own business," he said to me. "Take the horse and beat it."

'The two of them went off towards the Ponceau road, but by then I'd had time to put a name to that roughneck. It was young Mallart – his parents kept the Bistro des Sports in Petit-Louvigny. He was always hanging round the bar with his shoes undone and his cap over one eye. Believe me, he hasn't grown up a beauty. He's a nasty bit of work, and I know what I'm talking about. The police were after him for an armed robbery down in the south. I suppose he thought he'd be safe in his home town, or he may have been planning some dirty work round here. Anyway, he made a mistake hanging about here too long.'

'Why?' said Monsieur Douin uneasily.

'Sinet nabbed him last Thursday down by the station. Sinet hadn't forgotten his ugly mug either!'

Monsieur Douin rubbed his forehead. The red wine and old Blache's story had set his brain whirling. He began to wish he had never come. It was a fine thing when all he could discover was that Gaby's gang rode, twice a day, a wooden horse that had been the pride and joy of a crook's childhood.

'I've kept you the head,' the rag-and-bone man went on. 'It's somewhere under this pile of junk.'

'What head?' asked Monsieur Douin, dumbfounded.

'The horse's head, of course! I tried as best I could to stick it on, but it wouldn't hold. It's yours all the same – you can take it with you now; your kid will be pleased with it.'

Blache went and rummaged about at the other end of the hut. Soon he was back with something which Monsieur Douin recognized at once, though he had never set eyes on it before. Yes, it was the head that belonged to the three-wheeled horse. It was white, slightly reddened on the right-hand side. The nostrils were open and red, it had a row of menacing teeth, the eyes were set in an angry glare, and on its neck were the half-burnt remains of a black mane. The rag-and-bone man wrapped it in a sheet of newspaper, and after a last drink the two men parted.

'Well, I never,' said Monsieur Douin to himself as he walked back towards the station along the Ponceau road. The puffing and hissing of the passing engines, the flashing signal lights, the weird night scene of Le Triage helped to put things in their place in his mind. No, he wouldn't breathe a word to anyone, and the children could go on enjoying themselves as much as ever. The spoils-sports of yesterday evening? Lunatics! That was all there was to it!

'Our lad's not back?' he asked his wife.

'It's barely seven,' replied Madam Douin, without turning from the stove. 'Fernand's probably at Marion's house or Gaby's.'

'And the horse?' went on Monsieur Douin, suddenly becoming worried. 'They always bring it back as soon as it gets dark . . . there's something wrong.'

Madame Douin caught his feeling of anxiety.

'I've been in a quarter of an hour,' she answered, putting down a saucepan lid. 'If anything had happened the neighbours would have told me by now.'

'You stay here. I'm off to Madame Fabert's.'

He was out in a flash and striding down the rue des Petits-Pauvres. Not a light showed in Marion's home, and as soon as the twelve dogs saw Monsieur Douin coming up to the fence they started barking, but nobody moved in the house. Faster still he hurried along the rue de la Vache Noire, crossing to the left when he reached the main road. The short rue Aubertin was unlit and black as a tunnel, but fortunately a ray of light shone out from under the door of Monsieur Joye's house. Monsieur Douin went in to find his friend hurriedly taking off his working clothes. The children weren't there.

'I'm looking for Fernand,' stammered Monsieur Douin.

'And I'm looking for Gaby,' answered Monsieur Joye, slipping into his second-best coat. 'Haven't you heard the news?'

'What?' shouted Monsieur Douin, thoroughly alarmed.

'Their horse has been stolen!'

CHAPTER 3

Inspector Sinet

THE fine weather of the day before lasted until four o'clock. The blue sky made you think it was spring, and the sunshine set the grass on the Clos Pecqueux a-glitter. But by the time the children came out of school it had already grown overcast, the north wind beat down the smoke from the chimneys in the town, and little by little Louvigny took on its winter look – that foggy atmosphere in which Gaby's gang of ten most enjoyed the pleasure of being together and playing with their runaway horse.

Leaving Fernand and Zidore to fetch it out, Gaby had split the gang into two groups and sent them off to spy out the neighbourhood of the rue Petits-Pauvres. While the girls went down the hill to explore the rue de la Vache Noire, the boys patrolled the station, the alleys of Cité Ferrand, and the Square de la Libération. Marion on one side and Tatave on the other saw nothing suspicious and came back to say they could start.

Zidore had his two turns and then ran down the hill to mount guard on the finishing line. Then Gaby launched little Bonbon down the hill. Three minutes later the baby of the gang, out of breath, came up pushing the horse by the hind-quarters.

'Anything to report?' Gaby asked him.

'Not a cat stirring!' said Bonbon, 'but the mist's coming down on the railway tracks and you can hardly see the Ponceau road now.'

'Go down and stay with Zidore,' said Gaby. 'He'd better not be left alone. You can be his reserve.'

'Take Fifi with you,' added Marion. 'He only gets in our way here. Open the garden gate for him.'

As the boy and the little dog trotted off together, a friendly laugh from the older children followed them.

'I may be little, but I can look after myself,' shouted Bonbon, turning round with a fierce gesture.

Then from his blue smock he drew an enormous revolver that must have weighed at least four pounds. Gaby's jaw dropped.

'It doesn't work,' Tatave assured him proudly, 'but it must have been in the Franco-Prussian War; the muzzle's blocked with rust. From the distance you could scare people with it, though.'

'And from close up too!' said Gaby. 'I shouldn't like to get the butt between the eyes.'

It was Fernand's turn. He mounted the horse with that delightful shiver of fear and excitement which always brought your heart into your mouth just before you set off. The rue des Petits-Pauvres swept straight down to the crossroads at the rue Cécile, where the first lights were appearing in the shop windows. The dusk made the hill seem even steeper and the grimy houses on either side even taller. After that you had a blind turning, and then suddenly the wide horizon burst in front of you and gave you the feeling of flying into the air far above the earth that man and industry had laid waste.

The horse moved off, its wheels grinding out in protest, pushed by Juan and Mélie, who lent vigorous shoulders to the hind-quarters. At once Fernand raised his knees and got a good foot-hold on the rests on the front fork. As it moved down the slope the horse gathered speed.

'Now it's really going,' Fernand said to himself, gritting his teeth, 'but I shan't brake: it'll be just too bad if there's anything coming at the cross-roads.'

The rue Cécile was empty and the horse whizzed past like a bullet. Nose down to the handle-bars, the wind whistling past his ears, Fernand saw Monsieur Gall the cobbler as he went by, who gave him a cheerful smile, with his mouth full of nails. There was no one in the bend. 'This time I'll break the record,' Fernand thought. 'What a pity Zidore hasn't got the watch.'

Suddenly the end of the road, indistinct in a whitish mist, came to meet him, and beyond that the Clos Pecqueux with the Black Cow, a rusty phantom on the horizon. Zidore and little Bonbon were jumping up and down on the bank waving desperately to him. A car must be coming up the sunken road, but Fernand couldn't see it yet.

Taking fright, he braked hard with both feet, the hobnails in his boots sending up a shower of sparks from the roadway. It was effort wasted, the horse was going too fast. Next moment he was shooting up the short incline, shaving the bonnet of a van that was coming up the rue de la Vache Noire in low gear. A desperate heave on the handle-bars took him to the left. The front wheel bounced on the bank, the headless horse bucked like a real live one, and stood straight up on its two back wheels. Fernand was flung from the saddle, described a perfect curve above the barbed wire round the Clos, and fell flat on his face in the muddy grass.

'Quick, go and get Gaby and the others!' Zidore shouted to little Bonbon. 'And jump to it!'

Weak in the knees, and groggy from his fall, Fernand staggered to his feet. The van had pulled up thirty yards below with a shriek of brakes. The riderless horse, moving of its own accord, went slowly backwards down the slope, wobbling over the cobbles. The tarpaulin over the back of the van was up and the tailboard lowered. Two burly men were sitting on the floor with their legs hanging over the end. One of them was just about to get down, but the horse was coming by itself and they had only to reach out and grab it by the handle-bars as it came past.

Fernand and Zidore came up in time to seize one of the wheels and hang on with all their might, but the van was already moving off, and a fierce tug made them leave go, and flung them both to the ground. Fernand was the first to get up. Like a madman he chased the van as it vanished at full speed towards the main road.

'Thieves!' he cried through his tears, 'rotten thieves!'

A large stone made him stumble and he fell heavily at full length. After a moment he pulled himself up on his elbows and turned his head to watch the van plunge through the murk, turn sharp left, and disappear behind the trees along the main road. It was good-bye to the horse!

Zidore came up to comfort his friend. Putting his hands under his armpits, he heaved him to his feet.

Fernand's cheeks were deadly pale and tears glittered on them.

'Come on, cheer up!' said Zidore. 'They won't get away with it.'

Reinforcements came thundering down the rue des Petits-Pauvres and soon the whole gang came round the bend, boys and girls, hair flying, faces drawn, running neck and neck. Gaby, Tatave, and Juan at their head brandished long sticks torn from some fence.

'They didn't wait for you!' shouted Zidore pointing to the empty road. 'There were four of them. Two in the front seat and two in the back. They must have parked the van under the tunnel in Ponceau road – I bet one of them watched us from the top of the road. They let the horse come down three times running to put us off our guard, the rats! Fernand hadn't come out of the turn before the van was half-way up the hill. At a distance I didn't recognize either Pépé or Ugly behind the windscreen and I wasn't to know what would happen. Afterwards it was too late. Fernand went head over heels on the grass and the horse ran back down the slope on its own. They just picked it up with their little fingers.'

'You O.K.?' Marion asked Fernand.

'Quite,' he answered, choking back his tears.

'It's all my fault,' grumbled Gaby. 'We should have all been down here. Each one going up for his turn.'

'It would have come to the same thing,' said Zidore. 'They'd have pinched it as easily in front of Fernand's house.'

'Which way did they go?'

'That way.' Fernand pointed down the rue de la Vache Noire, which was gradually filling with mist.

For one long moment the ten stared in that direction,

fists clenched, their spirits as dismal as the damp, misty evening.

Fernand was still sobbing tears of pure rage.

'Those beasts ripped the horse out of our hands, and it wasn't worth a thing. It was a dirty trick. But I knew one of them: the same big brute as last night!'

'Ugly,' added Zidore. 'And wasn't he laughing!'

'They were wrong to attack us like that,' said Marion softly, weighing her words. 'They may have to pay dearly for it.'

'The horse could be worth a million pounds or a farthing,' cried Gaby. 'I'm not worried, it makes no odds. What matters is that it belonged to Fernand, to all of us, and they have stolen it from us!'

'You never know, we may find it again one day,' Marion went on in her sing-song voice. 'And then – I'll take good care they cry for help much longer than they did last time.'

'But what are we going to do?' demanded Berthe Gédéon plaintively.

'We're going to the police,' decided Fernand. 'And right away!'

'Steady on,' Zidore protested. 'That'll land us in a real mess: they'll just go on and on asking questions . . .'

'So what?' said Gaby. 'Look, we've done no harm. Our horse has been stolen and it's just a matter of finding the crooks who did it. That's what the police are paid for.'

Zidore shrugged. 'I know the cops: they just cause trouble, and you can't trust them an inch. They won't do a thing.'

'That's what you think! Anyway, even if they don't we'll have reported the robbery properly.'

'Who's coming with me?' demanded Fernand.

'We'll all go together,' Gaby decided. 'If you go on

your own it'll be a waste of time, the cops will just laugh at you. The superintendent will be much more impressed if he sees all ten of us arrive, and he won't slam the door in our faces. Horse-thieves aren't ghosts: we saw them. They've faces like everyone else – even if they're not very pretty. They've got to be caught!'

They walked back up to the cross-roads, talking it over among themselves, and turned down the rue Cécile. The Louvigny-Triage Police Station was on the ground floor of a new block three minutes' walk away. Fernand was in the lead, with Marion at his side, their hands firmly clasped. It was not to give him courage – he didn't lack that – rather to keep his anger hot so that he could say and do all he needed to.

'It's only another sort of game,' she reassured him, a smile in her grey eyes. 'Once you start it'll be all right.'

Half-way there they passed Father Brissard, the parish priest of Louvigny, who was very surprised to meet the procession.

'Where are you going?' he asked them.

Gaby told him the whole story. The kindly priest showed how sorry he felt, for he was very fond of the ten young ragamuffins from the rue des Petits-Pauvres. Some of them served as his altar boys, but only some: you could never trust a pair of jokers like Zidore and little Bonbon. Marion liked the priest too. She had managed to persuade him to give César a home when no one else would, because he ate too much. However, the parish priest of Louvigny had got much thinner since taking in the Great Dane, and it looked as though the dog were having the lion's share of the poor man's meals.

'It's not very nice to take their toy away from children who have hardly anything else,' said Father Brissard sadly, when Gaby had told him the whole story. 'Not at all nice. I only wish I could help you. But I'm not a policeman. Never mind, don't lose heart. You're much stronger than those criminals and you've got the advantage of numbers. All their wickedness can't frighten eleven resolute united children.'

'But there are only ten of us,' said Gaby.

'Eleven,' repeated Father Brissard with a smile. 'You can't see the eleventh, but he's always with you – a boy from Nazareth.'

Inspectors Sinet and Lamy were chatting in the untidy little office that served as their headquarters. It was a poky, windowless little den, cut off from the charge-room by a simple frosted-glass partition. On the other side were the sergeant on duty, two constables, and their evening's haul – a beggar of indeterminable age, sitting on a bench and monotonously telling his tale of woe.

'You know what I think, Lamy?' grumbled Inspector Sinet, 'we're just a bunch of down-at-heel, good-for-nothing, comic-opera policemen. Look at the cases we get: a grocer who wants us to keep his shop under observation because somebody helped themselves to a bit of cheese off the counter, an old lady in tears because the neighbour's cat has swallowed her canary.'

'You mustn't exaggerate,' sighed Lamy and drew at his pipe. 'Every now and then we do get a case that makes the headlines.'

Sinet slapped his thigh.

'Ah!' he cried. 'I was just waiting for you to say that. My dear chap, we never have the smallest hand in that sort of case: before you can say knife the high-ups take it right away from us. Listen, if you want any proof, what about that man Mallart I picked up near the station the other evening? They whisked him away before we had a chance to find out what he was up to in Louvigny. All I got out of it was this bruise on the cheek where he hit me.'

Gingerly he felt the plaster that ran like a scar across one side of his long face, which at this moment looked very bad-tempered. The two men were sprawled in their chairs, their feet carelessly resting on the dusty radiator in the office. Sinet had just come in with the tramp next door and still wore his bottle-green trench coat and his hat pushed back on his head. He was in a nasty mood.

'When you've done ten years on a suburban beat, as I have, you get to know what a gamble police work is. Why, you've as much chance of winning a big prize in the Lottery as you have of solving one of those nice fat cases that bring you promotion.'

'Poohoo,' said Lamy, sucking his pipe with a look of disbelief on his face.

'That's what it is – a lottery. You won't believe me? Well just cast your mind back – there's no need to go very far and you'll remember the three big prizes that have come up for the police in the last week: the hundred million francs on the Paris–Ventimiglia express, Frances Bennett's emeralds, and the gold bars from the Lévy-Bloch Bank. Honestly now, Lamy, do you really think we stand a chance? Of course not! It's always the same, our number never comes up.'

'Don't you complain,' sniggered Lamy, pointing with the stem of his pipe to his colleague's swollen face, 'this time you did get paid back!'

Inspector Sinet shrugged and laughed bitterly.

A crowd of people had just come into the charge-room; there was a confused murmur of voices with the grumpy tones of Sergeant Pécaut rising above them all. The two men, however, paid no attention.

'Even if the whole police force of Paris is on the three cases it doesn't mean we're out of the running in this god-forsaken dump,' replied Lamy obstinately.

'I'd like to know what we can do about it!' bellowed Sinet, getting really worked up. 'The hundred million from the Paris–Ventimiglia is the case of the century, and they won't solve it in a hurry. It was too well planned. Why, when the express got in on Wednesday night there were a dozen guards snoring their heads off on top of each other like a bunch of drunks, with the post-van reeking of chloroform.'

'All the same,' said Lamy quietly, 'we've a chance – granted, it's pretty slim.'

'How so?'

'The Paris–Ventimiglia express went through Louvigny–Triage, as it always does, right under your nose, Sinet!'

'So what? The lead-sealed sacks that held the money vanished into thin air between Dijon and Paris. Why, it's like looking for a needle in a haystack!'

'And Frances Bennett's emerald's?'

'Since when have you been going to tea at the Ritz, Monsieur Lamy?' he retorted, his little finger crooked and his voice taking on a most refined accent.

'O.K.,' said Lamy, 'but even so, the emeralds must have travelled since Thursday. What if you were to find them in one of those rag-and-bone men's huts?'

'We've no "fences" in the Faubourg-Bacchus,' answered Sinet positively. 'Go on, can you see old Blache carrying the film-star's jewels under that old hat of his?'

'You never know; the fruits of a robbery often end up in odd places, and often for the same reason. The crooks who carry out the theft either can't dispose of their loot or else when they come to split it they fall out and fight among themselves like mad dogs.'

The voices in the charge-room had risen and the two inspectors had to shout to make themselves understood. Suddenly Sergeant Pécaut pushed open the glass door.

'There's a bunch of kids out there who want to see Superintendent Blanchon,' he told Sinet. 'I can't make head or tail of their story. My two blokes have tried to clear them out, but there's a lot of them and they cling like limpets. Would you like to hear what they have to say?'

The Inspector brought his feet to the floor with a thud and winked at his colleague.

'What did I tell you?' he laughed. 'More work for us! Another story of the cat that killed the canary!'

Led by Gaby, the children filed quietly into the poky

little office. Sinet had righted his chair and was sitting squarely and majestically behind the ink-stained table.

'Well, what do you want?' he asked them sharply.

Pushed by Marion, Fernand stepped forward.

'We want to see Superintendent Blanchon,' he answered firmly.

'The Super's got plenty to do without seeing ten little urchins like you,' growled Sinet. 'It's my duty to lighten his work. Speak up!'

'We've come to make a charge,' Fernand went on, and the others nodded in agreement.

'What's the matter?' asked Sinet.

'The horse has been stolen,' declared Fernand, much as if it had been the Venus de Milo.

The two policemen seemed surprised. What was this? A horse?

'Which horse?' asked Sinet.

'The horse without a head,' answered Fernand in his innocence.

Sinet swallowed and stared hard at the ceiling, trying to hold back an awful impulse to laugh. Lamy was puffing away at his pipe in the corner, his feet on the radiator, his face bright scarlet; he was stifling his mirth.

Sinet lowered his eyes, rather put out by Fernand's closed scrutiny.

'A horse without a head? Really?' he repeated, keeping a straight face. 'There are horses of every description in Louvigny, but I've never seen one ambling around in that condition.'

'Ours is a horse on three wheels,' added Fernand. 'It's the only one we know in the rue des Petits-Pauvres.'

'Ah! I get you!' cried the Inspector, sitting back in his chair. 'Then your horse has been stolen. When did this happen?'

With some hesitation, Fernand told him of the conversation of the evening before and the curious offer to buy the horse.

Sinet took a clean sheet of paper from the drawer and put it all down just as it was told to him.

'Let's see . . . a horse without a head on three wheels . . . cross-roads of La Vache Noire . . . two men in fur-trimmed lumber-jackets . . . one answers to the name of Pépé, the other to the name of Ugly. He must be, too, if he lets them call him that!'

'He's horrible!' Bonbon declared in tones of outrage.

'Quite, quite!' said the Inspector. 'Go on, lad.'

After a moment or so, Sinet no longer felt he wanted to laugh, and the complicated story of the horse without a head had no small share in this sudden change of attitude. It was, after all, no more important than the mythical tale of the murdered canary, and yet the policeman was deeply touched by the attitude of the ten children so obstinately defending their own that they ventured into the one place that was so carefully, and with good reason, avoided by the youth of Louvigny. They looked to him to do something and it made Sinet rather sad, because he could see no way of solving this tangled mystery.

When Fernand had told his story he asked them: 'Did any of you take the number of the van?'

Fernand and Zidore could have kicked themselves; neither of them had thought of that. Excitedly little Bonbon raised his hand.

'I did, I saw the number!'

'Don't listen to him, mister!' said Tatave angrily. 'The little silly only knows ten letters and he always gets his numbers muddled.'

The children burst out laughing, and the two policemen exchanged a glance of amusement. Then Sinet went on with his questioning.

'Now, I want you to give me an exact description of the two crooks,' he told them. 'Tell me, in turn, what you thought they looked like – and mind you don't make anything up.'

All the descriptions agreed well enough, but it was Marion, speaking last, who put it in a nutshell.

'Ugly, the big one, had a face like a fox, and Pépé, the little one, a face like a bulldog: honestly, people always do look a bit like animals.'

'Well, that's helped things on!' sighed Sinet, and he pulled down his hat an inch or two to hide his face from Marion's cool glance.

For Inspector Sinet was definitely horse-faced. It was common knowledge, and all the policemen pulled his leg about it. He wondered whether the girl had noticed it already.

'What are you going to do' Gaby asked him.

'We'll have it thoroughly investigated,' declared the Inspector pompously. Promises cost him nothing. He indicated the paper. 'Here I have the beginning of a fine report, which I shall draw up right away. Tomorrow all the police in Louvigny will know your case down to the smallest detail and will be at work on it. Meanwhile go home quietly and sleep well. We'll find your horse for you.'

He felt himself blush for shame when he saw how quickly their faces brightened up and how the simple trust in him shone in their eyes.

'Oh, thank you, sir!' cried Gaby eagerly on behalf of the gang.

Gaily they filed out, ten pairs of boots ringing through the charge-room.

Inspector Lamy laughed as he lit up another pipe. 'You've certainly earned your day's pay,' he chuckled. 'Those kids will tell the world that Louvigny–Triage has the best detective in France.'

Sinet shrugged, screwed the piece of paper up and threw it into the waste-paper basket without another thought, when suddenly his face lit up. He plunged a hand into the basket, felt around, and pulled out his report. Carefully he smoothed it out on the table with the flat of his hand.

'What's up?' asked Lamy.

'I've seen that horse once before,' cried Sinet thoughtfully. 'Why, it even did me a wonderfully good turn! But for it I should never have caught that fellow the other night. You know! Mallart!'

It was Lamy's turn to show astonishment. 'But I thought you had no trouble picking him up?'

'No, but he was down already. He tripped over the horse in the dark. The kids had propped it against the wall. It must be the same one.'

'Well?' said Lamy, his interest thoroughly aroused. 'I can't see any connexion. Mallart's been under lock and key for the last five days; he couldn't have stolen the horse.'

'That's obvious,' agreed Sinet. 'Still, it's an odd coincidence, and I wonder if there isn't something serious behind it all. I'd like to get my hands on those two who think it a good joke to go round frightening those kids. Anyway, why steal the horse? The youngsters told us over and over again that it wasn't worth a thing.'

Lamy rubbed his hands. 'And now you're longing to know what was inside that horse. The hundred million from the Paris–Ventimiglia express? Frances Bennett's emeralds? Or perhaps the gold bars from the Lévy-Bloch

Bank? You've too much to choose from! Find the horse and then you'll know which to pick!'

Sinet shrugged his shoulders. 'That's nothing to do with it,' he said bitterly. 'Still, I think you could put in a nice bit of detective work if you went into the case.'

Just then there was the sound of a heavy tread in the charge-room. The agonized face of Sergeant Pécaut peered round the door.

'First the children, now their parents,' he announced. 'I've heard it all. Shall I send them in to you?'

'Yes,' groaned Sinet in despair.

The shy figures of Monsieur Joye and Monsieur Douin came through the door, both nervously twisting their railwaymen's caps in their hands.

'First of all, don't worry,' laughed the Inspector. 'We've had the kids dinning their story of the horse into our ears for the last hour. Couldn't get rid of them.'

'You must excuse them,' stammered Monsieur Douin, rather put out. 'You know they were very fond of that horse of theirs, Inspector; it was all they'd got. We're their parents and we can't afford to spend money on toys they'd only smash in a couple of days. Oh, they certainly put that horse through it.'

'What was it worth, by the way?' asked Sinet.

'Nothing,' said Monsieur Douin with a vague wave of the hand. 'Less than nothing, really.'

Then he told them how he had got the horse in the first place. But he kept quiet about the most important things: on the one hand the offer to buy the horse which he himself had, and what old Blache had told him about how he had found it – and on the other hand the queer way in which the cheap-jack Roublot had acted on market night, a few minutes after the young crook had been arrested at the corner of the rue des Petits-Pauvres. In this Monsieur

Douin was mistaken. The best of us can be dangerously misled by being too careful. As for Monsieur Joye, he didn't like the police anyway, so he just listened, nodded every now and then, and kept his mouth shut. The Inspector couldn't get anything more out of them, and he bade them good night with exaggerated politeness.

'Do you think you'll get the horse back,' asked Monsieur Douin, turning as he reached the door.

'We'll do our best,' Sinet assured him cheerfully. 'Louvigny isn't very big and if, as you say, the horse is quite worthless I expect we'll find it in someone's dustbin before long.'

He tried to take the matter lightly, but he couldn't forget that look of earnest appeal in Monsieur Douin's eye, and the children from the rue des Petits-Pauvres had put him out of countenance in the same way. It was the look that simple folk, who are attached to what little they have, give you when they are asking for it to be given back to them.

*

Fernand went straight back to the rue des Petits-Pauvres a few minutes ahead of his father. They key was in the lock and he pushed open the door, looked round the kitchen, where his mother was busy getting their supper, and then stopped dead in the doorway, with beating heart. There, fair and square on the table, was a horse's head that stared back at him with a sneer on its lips.

'Here you are at last!' sighed Madame Douin, as she gave him a kiss. 'We were beginning to get worried. Your father's been hunting high and low for you for the last half-hour. What on earth's been going on?'

'Our horse was stolen,' murmured Fernand, his eyes firmly fixed on the head.

No sooner had the horse vanished than its head appeared as if by magic in the Douin household. The old toy began to wear an air of mystery in Fernand's eyes, especially after he had been involved in the minor tragedy of its disappearance.

'Your father brought that ugly old thing home,' said Madame Douin when she saw where her son was looking. 'He called in on old Blache on his way home from Le Triage.'

Hearing the key turn in the lock, she turned round. It was Monsieur Douin. He seemed relieved to find his son at home, but there was a trace of ill humour in his usually good-natured face.

'You should have asked us before you made all that fuss,' he said to Fernand. 'What did you think you were doing, going down and worrying Inspector Sinet about an old horse that hadn't even got a head? I know it means a lot to you; but you don't just go off to the police like that. You should do things in the proper manner; why, you'll make us the laughing-stock of the district!'

'Those two blokes didn't pinch the horse for fun,' answered Fernand angrily. 'They looked as though they were after something much more valuable than just a broken old toy.'

All unaware, he had set this little incident in its true light. He had discovered a truth of which Monsieur Douin had had a vague inkling after his talk with old Blache, and of which Inspector Sinet still refused to believe the existence.

Madame Douin made them tell her the whole story, and when she had heard it all she was highly indignant.

'Well, if that isn't the limit! Fancy anyone stealing their toys from poor children – it's shameful. Why, you wouldn't believe it if you saw it in the papers. Honest to goodness, some people haven't a heart!'

Fernand went straight up to bed after supper. He lay awake in the dark listening to the whistles of the passing trains through the thin walls of his little bedroom. At that very moment, in eight other homes, his friends were asking themselves the same puzzling questions, and going over in their minds the events of the day in their smallest detail.

In the next room, Monsieur Douin, rather tired, was feeling the ardour which had made him take up arms for the children in the loss of their treasure grow somewhat colder.

'Do you think the police will do anything?' his wife asked him.

'Can't say. If they don't find it, it'll be just too bad. A good riddance, anyway: that horse was beginning to get on my nerves!'

CHAPTER 4

A Rusty Key

THE next evening it was raining so hard that Gaby's gang had to split up when they came out of school. Fernand went home with Marion to the bottom of the rue des Petits-Pauvres. Before they parted she said to him:

'You know, we'll have to find something to make up for the horse. Something must be done. If we all break up after school every day, before long there won't be a gang left, and that would be a shame. At the minute there aren't ten other kids in the place who stick together as we do.'

Fernand nodded agreement. At the end of the garden he could hear Marion's twelve dogs whimpering with excitement.

'Would you like me to train one for you?' she suggested with a laugh. 'Then you wouldn't feel so much on your own in the house.'

'Mum wouldn't let me,' Fernand answered. 'She doesn't like animals, and anyway the house isn't really big enough for the three of us as it is.'

'Oh, she'd get used to it,' said Marion. 'Besides, if you've a good dog in the house it makes people think twice about breaking in.'

They said good-bye, and she pushed open the gate. Fernand hurried away up the road in his old mackintosh, the hood over his head and the tail slapping against his legs like a wet fish. His mother had given him a key, and he carelessly left it on the outside of the door when he came in. He shook the raincoat, pulled out the damper in the stove, and dumped the heavy canvas bag he used as a satchel on the table. Then, feeling a draught on the back of his legs, he looked over his shoulder at the door. It was slightly open, and so he got up to shut it. But something was in the way, and looking down, Fernand saw with a start that there was the toe of a shoe wedged in the crack.

Slowly he let the door open, his heart came into his mouth, and he suddenly felt frightened. Roublot the cheap-jack was standing on the front step. A little stream of water ran down from the brim of his beret, he had a fixed grin on his face, and under his arms was a large, square parcel carefully wrapped and securely tied. He came in, with a sharp movement drew the key from the lock, closed the door, and double-locked it from the inside.

'I've just come to pay you a friendly little visit,' he said, turning to Fernand. 'Come here.'

Fernand backed to the opposite end of the room and took refuge behind the table. He was wild at letting himself be caught so easily. His parents wouldn't be back before six; Gaby and the others might be anywhere in town, and Marion lived too far away to hear him if he called for help. Fortunately, though he was big and strong, Roublot had none of the frightening self-possession of the men in the van. He was a coward at heart. Fernand kept his eyes on him.

'I'm not afraid of you,' he said, making himself sound as cheeky as he could. 'But it isn't often we see your ugly mug around here except Thursdays. If it's the horse you're after, you needn't waste your time. It was pinched yesterday evening.'

'I know,' Roublot answered calmly. 'Rotten for you, wasn't it? Well, no need to make a song and dance about

it; come and see what I've brought you.'

He put his parcel on the table and very slowly started to unwrap it, peering all the while into the dark corners of the room. Fernand never took his eyes off him.

'I know the horse has gone, but it'll come back,' he declared. Trying to find out how the land lay, he added, 'The police were told an hour after it was stolen. Inspector Sinet's written a report on it, a proper one too, with a description of the thieves and everything! They won't get away with it!'

Roublot's gaze wandered, and Fernand knew his thrust had gone home. The cheap-jack lowered his head to hide his annoyance, pulled back the paper, and revealed an expensive-looking red and green box.

'It's an electric train,' he said with a friendly smile. 'There are some decent folk in Louvigny, after all. The market people heard what happened last night, and so they clubbed together and bought it for you. They got me to bring it to you: wasn't that nice of them?'

But Fernand was unmoved. He edged his way towards the stove, one hand behind his back feeling for the poker.

'The train's for you, you and the others,' said Roublot engagingly. 'Come on, let's both put the rails together and you can try it out right away.'

'Phoo!' retorted Fernand contemptuously. 'Me and my friends are too old to play at that kid's game. If we want trains we've real ones on the tracks at the other side of the road. You'd better pack up your rubbish, I wouldn't touch it!'

Roublot darted round the table, fists clenched. Fernand leapt aside and took his stand in the hallway, poker in hand.

'One more step and you'll get this in the face!' he said, his lips white with anger. 'I won't miss! This is my house and I'm looking after it.'

Sweat and rain trickled down Roublot's sallow face. Almost automatically he wrapped up his parcel again. His rat's eyes darted desperately round the room. He stepped back towards the sink. Keeping one eye fixed on the boy, he opened both the cupboards, rummaged round the dresser, had a quick look into the clothes cupboard, the coal-scuttle, and the bread-bin, and passed his hand swiftly and skilfully among the shelves. It only took him a couple of minutes to explore every nook and cranny, and in his keenness he even cast an eye over the ash-can. Then he turned sharply towards the boy. Fernand took a firmer hold on the poker.

'I don't know what you've come to find,' he said quietly. 'We've no valuables in the place. The only thing that you'd be interested in is hanging on the coat-rack behind you. Lift up the mackintosh and take a look. I don't want you to have all this trouble for nothing!'

Roublot tugged the waterproof aside and gave a muffled exclamation. He gaped at the staring eyes and grinning teeth of the horse's head, which had been mounted on a board, like a big-game trophy. Roublot wiped his forehead and with a worried look opened the door and dashed out. A mocking laugh rang in his ears as he fled towards the Square.

Fernand shut and double-locked the door, then he opened his school books, and, though his hand still trembled, sat down to write out his homework.

Five minutes later there was a knock. His heart jumped.

'Open up,' said a deep voice. 'Quick!'

Fernand took up the poker and tiptoed to the door.

'Who's there?' he asked, disguising his voice.

'Inspector Sinet.'

Fernand was very relieved and opened the door wide, standing back to let the policeman in.

'What was Roublot after?' Sinet asked him without further ado.

'Nothing!' Fernand replied nervously. 'He just came to bring me a present to make up for the horse.'

Carefully the Inspector closed the door.

'None of those fairy stories,' he said harshly. 'You can't tell me you show anyone out at the end of a poker when that's all he's come for. I was outside, and I saw it all through the window. Well, then?'

Fernand dropped his head. 'He seemed to be after something,' he admitted. 'If he'd got me to play with the train he'd have been over the house from top to bottom. But I didn't let him take me in.'

'He might have found ways of doing that,' said the Inspector.

'I thought so too; I really was in a bit of a fix.'

'You've no idea, though, just what he was after?' asked Sinet, staring around him with curiosity.

'None at all. There's nothing valuable in this house, and Mum always keeps the housekeeping money on her.'

'But why didn't you want the train?'

'It all seemed a bit odd to me. The market people couldn't care less about our horse. Why, they've never even set eyes on it!'

'You were right,' said Sinet, laughing. 'This fellow Roublot's not the sort of person you want to have anything to do with. Did you know he'd already been to prison?'

'No, but you can tell what he's like by his face. I bet he'll go again.'

Sinet lit a cigarette and took a good look round the room. 'Do you think I could have a look round?' he asked Fernand abruptly.

The boy answered him with a smile. 'You're different. Come on, I'll show you over the house.'

Sinet seemed a little ill at ease. 'Don't tell your parents,' he warned him. 'It's a bit irregular, I shouldn't really do a thing like this without a proper search warrant. There may be something here . . . you don't know how important it is, but I've a sharp pair of eyes, and I may be able to spot it right away.'

'I get you, but it's nothing more to do with the horse?' said Fernand rather disappointedly.

'On the contrary,' Sinet flashed back at him, 'the horse was the start of it all. Maybe those two who stole the horse made a mistake and didn't get what they wanted.'

'Oh, I hadn't thought of that.'

With Fernand to guide him, the Inspector went slowly through the house. He made no bones about ferreting through the drawers and cupboards.

By the time Sinet had passed from his parents' room to his own, Fernand was watching him with bated breath. He wouldn't have been a bit surprised if he had pulled a diamond as big as a hen's egg from under his pillow.

'There's nothing here,' sighed Sinet angrily. 'Let's go back to the kitchen.'

Having gone through Monsieur Douin's tool-box with the same lack of success, Sinet lit a cigarette butt, leaned back against the table, and sat Fernand down facing him.

'If I didn't know what a straight man your father was,' he said gravely, 'I'd have been thinking all sorts of funny things. Are you going to tell him about the visitors you've had this evening, Roublot and me?'

Fernand shook his head. 'No,' he said firmly. 'He has enough to think about already with his job. So long as there's nothing shady about all this, there's no point in giving him anything more to worry about.'

'Good,' said the Inspector, smiling to himself. 'You know how to take responsibility, anyway. Listen carefully, my lad. You're no fool. If you find out anything you think will interest me when you're knocking around, just you let me know; and as for Roublot, don't worry, I'll keep an eye on him.

'So shall we,' declared Fernand, looking as though he meant business.

*

As usual, Roublot drove up in his new van at about ten o'clock. Time didn't matter to him.

It had been snowing since the early morning, a few scattered flakes, which fell slowly and melted as soon as they touched the dirty pavements. Clouds of white smoke from Le Triage rose in a thick column above the station, against the grey, lowering sky. Roublot had set up his stall and began to bawl out the virtues of his 'Simplex Super Chipper' to catch the housewives of Louvigny. Oh, it was certainly a first-class instrument, adopted by the War Office too, and it could chip a bushel of potatoes in two minutes twenty point six seconds!

Every now and then he would turn round and glance towards the steamy windows of the Café Parisien. Twenty or so market idlers honoured his demonstration with their presence and he managed to get rid of a couple of his 'Chippers'. Then his audience gradually slipped away and exposed a second row of spectators, who doubtless awaited another demonstration.

As he looked up, Roublot felt his heart miss a beat. There were the ten lined up in front of him in order of height. They were on their best behaviour, standing quite still, and they didn't say a word. Bernard Joye, tall for his age, fresh-faced, an old cap pulled down across his brown hair; Zidore Loche, blue with cold, acres of a sweater several sizes too large for him flapping round his skinny frame and coming nearly down to his knees; Fernand Douin, slim and fair-haired, his blue beret pulled down to his ears; Tatave Louvrier, so fat that he seemed to be bursting out of the patched and darned red cloth windbreaker he wore; Juan Gomez, muffled up in a short coat with its moth-eaten velvet collar turned up to his ears and a knitted cap pulled down over his black gipsy hair; Marion Fabert, stiff and straight under her long man's jacket, her fair hair pulled under her black beret, making her pale face look quite stern; Berthe Gédéon, slim and pretty, in a dreadful red pullover with enormous stitches which she had knitted herself; Mélie Babin, wrapped up in a black shawl which set off the brightness of her smile and the gleam of her fringe of golden hair; Criquet Lariqué, thin and shivering in spite of his thick padded jacket with its fur collar – and last, at the end of the row, Bonbon Louvrier, the baby of the gang, encased in many thicknesses of woollen jerseys under his blue smock and tied up in a long scarf that went twice round his neck and was tied across his chest like a cross-belt.

There, then, stood the ten and watched Monsieur Roublot. They weren't in the least bit cheeky; they just stared at him, that was all. The cheap-jack tried at first to pass it off with a laugh and hailed them cheerfully.

'Glad to see you again,' he called, with a forced smile.

'Come over here; you look as though you all like a nice plate of chips, I'll give another demonstration just for you.'

Not one of them moved. They were rooted to the pavement. Their breath floated lightly above their heads in a white cloud of steam. Now and then the wind blew a flurry of snowflakes in front of their set faces. They were watching Roublot, and Roublot soon felt himself caught by their stares. He tried to shake himself free and cried his wares at the top of his voice, slicing up half a bushel of potatoes at the same time. But he didn't succeed. No one came to see how the 'Simplex Super Chipper' worked, and the ten still watched him with uncanny patience, hardly moving an eyelid.

Suddenly Roublot lost his temper. 'Get out!' he yelled. 'Get out, you blasted kids!'

But they didn't move an inch. Their gaze softened a little and became even more attentive. In spite of the cold, Roublot felt the sweat gather on his forehead.

'Right,' he said threateningly. 'Well, if you won't, don't move on – then you'll all share a good cuff of the ears. Don't worry, I've enough to go round.'

Still no one, from Gaby to Bonbon, broke the line. People came up and looked over their shoulders to see what they were staring at, and inevitably their looks fell on Roublot's face, whose pallor was no longer that of anger, but of fear. Fear of what? Folk looked blankly to their right and their left and then back at Roublot as hard as the children. Policeman Ducrin, who was patrolling the market with two of his colleagues, came up on his beat at that moment. The silence of it all surprised him.

'What are you looking at?' he asked Gaby.

Gaby didn't answer, and Ducrin followed the direction

of his stare. He found himself face to face with a very frightened Roublot, who now had the policeman to add to his other watchers. In fact, Roublot had never drawn a crowd like this before; nevertheless he set to at dismantling his 'Super Chipper', and threw the pieces pell-mell into his cases.

'He looks proper poorly, poor man!' said a concierge from Cité Ferrand, who expected him to pass out before her eyes. 'It's this wicked cold; it freezes your blood, it reelly does!'

But Roublot didn't pass out. He packed up his trestle-table at break-neck speed and bundled all his gear into the back of his van. Trembling with rage, he turned to the children, but as he opened his mouth the words stuck in his throat, for little Bonbon came curveting out of their ranks astride an old spade ornamented with a horse's head.

'Gidee up! Gidee up!' cried Bonbon, clattering his heels and the iron spade.

Pulling on imaginary reins, he brought the horse's head up to meet the concentrated glare that Roublot cast upon him. The crowd burst out laughing, and the ten children, suddenly relaxing, joined in. Roublot fled, leapt into his van like a madman, and drove off at top speed.

'That's paid him,' said Marion; 'that'll teach him to shove his way into other's people's houses. The least we could do was to return his call.'

'That evens things up,' added Fernand. 'But he must have a jolly guilty conscience to dash off like that.'

Gaby, Fernand, and Zidore then strolled over towards the Café Parisien, whose windows were already throwing a rosy light into the fast-gathering darkness. The three children glanced in. Some of the market people, blowing on their frozen fingers, were standing at the bar, but the room itself was empty.

'Juan, you come back this way in an hour or two to see if Roublot returns,' said Gaby. 'If he does we'll do the same act again, and if that doesn't shift him, Marion can introduce a couple of her big dogs to him. Meanwhile we've got to get this shed at the saw-mill straight. It's just the place for us.'

Marion had discovered the spot when she was exploring the patchwork of overgrown gardens and tumble-down houses that lay between the rue des Petits-Pauvres and the main road crossing the rue de la Vache Noire. You turned up a narrow path on the left, that ran between the ruins of the old hospital and the fence beside Van den Berg's coal-yard. This was Lilac Lane. True, the coal-dust had killed off the original lilacs years ago, but their memory was preserved by the lane, a cut winding between high walls until it brought you to the disused saw-mill, whose empty and crumbling buildings backed on to the rue Cécile. Their best plan, then, was to get in by this hidden entrance. It was just the place they had always wanted, a wooden shed, strongly walled on three sides, but on the fourth opening southwards on to an overgrown yard. It was empty, but the scent of sawn wood still lingered, and from the first moment that she poked her nose inside, Marion realized that this forgotten corner, where the noise of the trains could hardly be heard, would be the very place for the gang to hold its meetings.

Fernand and Marion were the first to get there, to set to rights 'our club', as Gaby already somewhat pompously called it. The ground was carpeted with a thick layer of rotting sawdust into which one's feet sank. Fernand had to dig deep to get down to solid earth, and when he had done so he dug out a little square fireplace which he enclosed with flat stones. Meanwhile Marion explored the empty workshops, Fifi at her heels.

First she brought back some planks, then two trestles, a packing-case which was still fairly sound, two saucepans, some tins, a bucket, a poker, a coal shovel, and ten billets of oak for seats, one for each of them. There was no need to worry about fuel, for there were stacks of good dry wood all round.

It was four o'clock by the time Fernand got the fire alight and its flames soon glowed red upon the walls of the old shed. Their light marked out a little corner of cosy warmth, with the seats set in a circle round the hearth, the packing-case cupboard on one side proudly displaying its saucepans, the trestle-top on the other, and the poker stuck into the ground like a sword beside the fire.

Gaby, Zidore, and Mélie came in as night fell. They drew a sharp breath of pleasure when they saw the 'club' all ready for them, the fire throwing a host of dancing shadows on the walls.

'I've kept your seats for you,' Marion told them. 'Every one has the name of its owner chalked on it.'

'We've brought the grub,' answered Gaby. 'There's not a lot, but it should keep the wolf from the door.'

Whereupon he took a meat cube and eight rather battered potatoes out of his pockets and lined them up on the table.

'Well, I've only got one but at least it's a decent size,' said Zidore; and to the delight of his friends he produced an enormous muddy potato that must have weighed a good pound.

'I can't put it with the others,' laughed Fernand. 'It would take a couple of hours to cook; we'll save it for later.'

Marion put a saucepan of water on the fire to boil for the soup, and soon Tatave and Bonbon came in, black as sweeps from head to foot.

'We mistook the door into the coal-yard for the way in here,' Tatave explained. 'Bonbon fell into the dust-pit and I had to pull him out. What a life!'

Not far behind them was Berthe Gédéon, hand in hand with Criquet Lariqué. The darky rolled his eyes in amazement at the glories of the hide-out.

'I've brought you all a present,' he declared, pulling a somewhat tattered little packet out of his coat.

It was the first time this had happened. They all held their breath, their eyes glued to the scrap of newspaper Criquet was so carefully unrolling. From it he produced a cigarette, and although it had got a bit wet, he ceremoniously passed it round, watching his friends' faces as he did so. They gave him a terrific reception.

Juan came last, slipping in like a shadow, his wool cap pulled down over his ears, for the snow was falling more and more thickly. He brought bad news.

'Roublot hasn't come back to the market-place,' he reported, warming his hands over the fire; 'but his van's parked in the rue des Alliés, and he must be somewhere in the area right now.'

His news cast a chill. Marion said nothing, but turning to the far end of the shed, she gave a low whistle. Two great black dogs, that no one had noticed before, came out of the darkest corner, their eyes sparkling like rubies in the firelight. They lay down at her feet, their heads in her lap.

'Butor and Fanfan,' murmured Marion. 'The two best watch-dogs in Louvigny-Cambrouse. I'll bring them with me every time the club meets. Roublot can try to get round them with a pound of sausages if he likes, but they'll have the seat of his trousers all the same; just look at their teeth.'

These were duly admired from a safe distance, and the children's gaiety returned. Berthe and Mélie skilfully and speedily served up the food, and soon the ten of them were sipping their cans of steaming soup.

'I've never tasted better,' sighed Tatave, licking his lips.

It was only one rather stale beef cube dissolved in a saucepan of water, but it became indescribably delicious when they drank it together and in secret in the wooden shed. Gaby lit the cigarette and passed it round like a pipe of peace. Marion and Fernand set the potatoes to bake in the ashes. Little by little the flames died down, until all that was left was the glowing heart of the fire that burned up now and then to light the circle of motionless figures around it. No one spoke: the two dogs whimpered with delight, but didn't even dare to scratch.

'What are we going to talk about?' asked Marion at last.

'The horse, naturally,' said Gaby. 'We'll go round in turn and each say what he thinks, even the kids. Let's start with Fernand. He should know more about it than any of us.'

All eyes were turned on young Douin.

'One thing that's really struck me,' said Fernand, choosing his words, 'is that for a whole year, when we must have had four hundred rides on that horse, not a soul took a scrap of notice. Then all of a sudden everyone seems to be interested in it, just as though at one moment it was worth nothing and then at another it suddenly became worth a lot.'

The children around the fire shifted nervously. The first opinion looked like being very interesting.

'Good,' said Gaby. 'Now we've got to find out when

that moment was. That's the root of it all. I think everything began that evening the horse lost its front wheel, and more exactly when Roublot started hanging round you and Marion. What happened before and after that?'

'I've told you already,' Fernand answered. 'When we got back from the market I found the horse lying in the gutter, so I picked it up and leant it up against the wall again. Then the ruffian came up and . . .'

'Roublot had his eye on the horse,' interrupted Marion. 'I'm certain we were in his way.'

'And after that?' Gaby went on.

'After that, Dad came home,' Fernand replied. 'We took the wheels off, and next day the horse was taken away for repair. I can't think of anything else to tell you. Nothing mysterious happened at home.'

'Mysteries just come of their own accord,' laughed Zidore; 'you can't account for them. Perhaps your horse had started to lay golden eggs round the place.'

The gang glared at him.

'Stop fooling,' said Fernand angrily. 'You all know as well as I do that the horse wasn't worth a bean, ever. Last night, after Roublot's visit, the Inspector said something that made me prick me ears up.'

'What?' asked Gaby.

'Sinet said to me, "Maybe those fellows in the van took the horse all for nothing: made a mistake." That would explain why Roublot searched the house.'

Zidore and Gaby gave a low whistle, while the others just stared at each other, uncomprehendingly.

'And so,' said Gaby dreamily, 'if the cheap-jack's in league with that mob, he hoped to find something in your house that's worth an awful lot to them. That alters it all! The horse let them down, but the Douins' house still interests them.'

'Roublot didn't find anything,' Fernand protested, rather overwhelmed.

'Perhaps he didn't know what he was looking for,' laughed Mélie.

'All this is getting us away from the horse,' said Marion. 'But there's one thing we do know: the night of the smash the horse suddenly became worth an awful lot to a lot of people, and five days later, on the night it was stolen, it was worth nothing at all. You've got to admit that the horse must somehow have changed in that time.'

'And that was either when it was in Fernand's hands or his father's – or else in Monsieur Rossi's workshop,' Gaby concluded. 'No one else could have touched it.'

Although the fire was slowly dying, Fernand saw the eyes of the children light up round him. Marion was gently stroking her dogs, but she too was watching him. Everyone waited with bated breath for what he had to say. Gaby came to his rescue.

'There's still something that's slipped your mind,' Gaby said kindly. 'It could happen to anyone. Try to remember.'

'Monsieur Rossi only cut off the old fork and put on a new one,' said Fernand, shaking his head. 'That angle's no good. When we sent him the horse it was dismantled and there was nothing missing when he let us have it back.'

'Are you quite sure?' asked Zidore. 'Even if Monsieur Rossi didn't touch it, your father could easily have taken a bit away without your noticing.'

'I was there,' said Fernand, 'and I helped him from start to finish. We took off the wheels, screwed the nuts back, and scraped a bit of rust off odd places.'

'Nothing else?'

'Oh yes! Dad took the horse by its hind legs and

emptied it out on the hall floor. The belly was jammed full, and Dad didn't want to take it to Monsieur Rossi in that state.'

'That's it!' shouted Gaby, jumping up. 'What was in the horse?'

'You know as well as I do,' laughed Fernand. 'You were always shoving any old junk you could find down his neck, poor old horse!'

Gaby leant over Fernand.

'You great oaf!' he cried shaking him. 'There must have been something in the horse that you didn't notice. You let it get lost. What did you get out of the horse?'

Fernand caught on. Staring in front of him, he tried to relive every detail of that evening.

'First of all there was cotton waste and oily rags corking up the hole in the neck,' he said tonelessly. 'Dad had to take a hook to clear them out. Then all the rest came tumbling out.'

'What?'

'Rusty old iron. The horse must have had a good twenty pounds of it inside.'

'What sort of old iron?' Gaby asked insistently.

'Bolts, a broken file, a door-knob.'

'I shoved that in,' Zidore had to admit, 'with the other junk. The horse sounded a bit hollow. He needed weighting.'

'Dad put the door-handle aside to use in the house,' added Fernand; 'it wasn't all that bad.'

'What else?'

'A bit of old chain, a hook, two sardine-tins, a curtain ring, an alarm clock, half a pair of pliers, a bed spring, an old tin mug, an old key.'

As each item was mentioned it was acknowledged by the member of the gang who had contributed towards the clatter that came from the horse as it shot down the hill. (A clatter that had increased the riders' pleasure tenfold.) But no one seemed to have any recollection of the key. There was a dead silence.

'Who put the key in the horse?' yelled Gaby, glaring angrily at the astonished faces round the glowing fire.

The children stared round-eyed and speechless at each other. No one moved a muscle.

'Well, the key didn't get inside the horse on its own,' said Marion in her sing-song voice. 'If none of us put it there, someone outside the gang must have done. We've recognized all the other things, so there's no point in going any further: the key's the only thing that could have made the horse worth anything!'

'What was it like?' Gaby asked Fernand.

'A long one like a garage key, all rusty, with a wooden label on the end.'

'What did your father do with it?'

Fernand thought for a bit before he answered. 'I'm not quite sure,' he said, 'but I think he must have hung it up without thinking, under the electric meter along with the keys of the house.'

Gaby poked the fire and the flames sprang up again lighting up the circle of faces. The smell of roast potatoes mingled with the scent of pine resin. Tatave cleared the cinders off one and stuck the point of is knife into it.

'Done to a turn!' he said, with immense satisfaction.

'The spuds can wait,' retorted Gaby. 'We've much more important things to do first.'

He turned to Fernand. 'Come on,' he said sharply. 'Back to your place as fast as we can go. *We've got to get that key at all costs!*'

Outside, it was snowing so hard that you could scarcely see more than a few yards in front of you. The two boys hurried up the rue des Petits-Pauvres, their footfalls muffled in the carpet of flakes that grew thicker every minute. Occasionally the dim light of a small shop window would fall on a solitary passer-by. Fernand saw no suspicious shadows lurking at the street corner. He opened the door and tiptoed over to the window to draw the curtain.

'Turn on the light!' he hissed at Gaby.

Then the two boys tumbled over each other into the hall. A dozen keys, some gleaming, some tarnished, hung in a jumble below the meter, and among them a long one with a wooden label fastened to it by a piece of copper wire.

'That's it,' said Fernand eagerly, 'I remember it now.'

'Well, there's nothing very odd about it,' said Gaby, weighing it in the palm of his hand. 'It looks just the same as any other key. Hang on, though! There's some writing on the label.'

'Don't let's hang about too long,' answered Fernand. 'We'll have bags of time to have a good look at it when we get back to the shed.'

When they returned they found the gang sharing out the potatoes. Zidore had thrown some dry shavings on the embers. The flames crackled up and the glow made their shadows dance on the walls. By the light of the fire they examined the key. The wooden label had some writing on it, though the ink had faded a bit and wasn't easy to read.

'Billette Works, 224 Ponceau Road,' was what Gaby made out. Astonished, he asked: 'Does that mean anything to anyone?'

Marion knew the handful of factories and workshops between the Clos Pecqueux and the railway tracks well enough.

'Number 224's just the other side of the little tunnel,'

she said. 'It's that grey concrete block next door to César Aravant's goods-yard. The Billette factory has been closed since the war. I've never seen a soul round there.'

'Well, what did they make?' asked the curious Gaby.

Marion shrugged to show she didn't know.

'We'll find out tomorrow,' was all she said; 'we've got the key.'

CHAPTER 5

The Abandoned Factory

INSPECTOR SINET could only spare odd moments for the case of the stolen horse. He did so more from his own interest than through any sense of duty, for Superintendent Blanchon passed it off as a dubious practical joke in which it would be easy for the police to make utter fools of themselves.

The men who had planned the theft of the horse seemed to have disappeared into the maze of back streets of the little factory town, where there was no lack of good hiding-places. Sinet and Lamy had made discreet inquiries among the rather mixed crowd of the market place. Nobody had heard of Ugly or Pépé there – at least, not by those nicknames.

Then again, it was no easy matter to get on Roublot's tracks. He had the van at his disposal, and except on market day it was only occasionally that you saw him in Louvigny, and you could never tell in advance just when that would be. All that remained were the children, who could be easily watched at any hour of the day without arousing their suspicions. And here too Sinet suddenly drew blank. Day after day Gaby's gang vanished from its usual haunts. Every evening between six and seven the rue des Petits-Pauvres was as dismal and as silent as the grave. But the Inspector was not to be put off his apparently useless investigation. He was convinced that the children, quite unknown to themselves, had got caught up in some crime, and had become the object of the gang's deepest interest, although the crooks themselves were careful to keep well in the background.

'Something happened in Louvigny last Wednesday night,' he said to Lamy one evening, 'and no one here realizes how important it was.'

They pored over the thick sheaf of daily bulletins which summarized the activities of the police during the fateful week. But there was nothing. Sinet had been right when he had said that Louvigny hadn't drawn the lucky number. On the Tuesday, Frances Bennett had been relieved of her emeralds as she stepped out of the Ritz, and on Thursday the armour-plated van from the Lévy-Bloch Bank had deposited its thirty gold bars worth sixteen million francs in a quiet side street.

'But the hundred million francs vanished from the Paris–Ventimiglia express that night,' observed Lamy, whose broad red face had by now lost its mocking grin.

Sinet shook his head in frank disbelief. 'The business of the horse doesn't hide a master crime like that,' he said, shrugging his shoulders. 'As I see it, it's only some piece of petty pilfering; you always get it round the sidings. Somewhere in the area there's an old shed they must use to hide the stolen goods: twenty bags of mouldy flour, a cask of rough wine, a roll of shoddy cloth, all sorts of wretched little things taken on the sly in the confusion of loading and unloading – the thieves have an awful job to get rid of them. There's no more in it than that, I'd say.'

Just then Sergeant Pécaut peered round the door. 'This lady has something interesting to tell you,' he said, showing in a gentle little old woman in black.

From the way she clasped and unclasped her hands, Sinet, to his dismay, thought that it was another clear case of the brutal murder of a canary. But he was wrong.

'I live in an alley off the rue Cécile,' said the little old woman, without beating about the bush; 'it's a quiet neighbourhood, but I don't want to go up like a bonfire one of these nights.'

'Why?' asked Sinet, amazed.

'For the last two days,' she answered, 'somebody's been up to tricks, lighting a fire in a shed in the saw-mill. I didn't like to tell all the neighbours, it's none of their business – I just thought I'd warn you.'

'We'll look into it right away,' Sinet promised her. 'You just go home and don't worry about the fire any more.'

When the little old woman had gone, he slipped on his trench coat and strode out into the bitter night, leaving Lamy on duty.

The abandoned saw-mill had only one opening on to the rue Cécile, and that was a tall pair of iron gates, securely chained together. It was the work of a moment for Sinet to force the massive padlock and then, switching on his torch, he felt his way as best he could among the maze of buildings, stumbling now and then on the rotten baulks of timber that cluttered the yards and pathways.

Soon, as far as he could judge, he thought he had reached the fence that ran parallel to the alley in which the old lady lived. Suddenly the Inspector saw the furtive glow of a fire reflected on the planks heaped up in abandon, half filling the yard. The light came from a wooden shed. It was strong enough to pick out the clumps of weed that sprouted up from the ground, and Sinet didn't risk discovery by walking into the open. Slowly he crept from pile to pile, and soon found himself in front of the entrance. From there he could see right into the shed, but what he saw made him doubt his senses.

Ten figures were seated around a camp fire, in enormous carnival masks, and the leaping flames seemed to give a weird life to their cardboard faces and make their expressions more frightening or comic than they really were. In their midst, before the blaze, a poker surmounted by a horse's head stood like a totem-pole.

The masked forms were passing round a large roast chicken, browned to a turn, whose plumpness did not escape Sinet, far away as he was. From his hiding-place he could hear only a dull murmur of voices, but the meeting seemed to be a stormy one, for it ended with one of the figures grabbing the chicken by the leg and booting it to the other end of the shed. The chicken hit the wall with a dull thud and bounced back into the sawdust. All at once the masks split into two teams and a furious and confused game of football began, in which the chicken was used as the ball. Suddenly a tall mask, who seemed to be the captain, broke through the opposing side and dribbling forward, shot the chicken out of the door. It landed in the yard within a few feet of Sinet.

The chicken too was only cardboard, and had already lost a drumstick in the scrimmage. The Inspector couldn't take his eyes off the scene, and thought he had stepped into another world. He didn't move, which was just as well, because two huge black dogs were on watch in Lilac Lane.

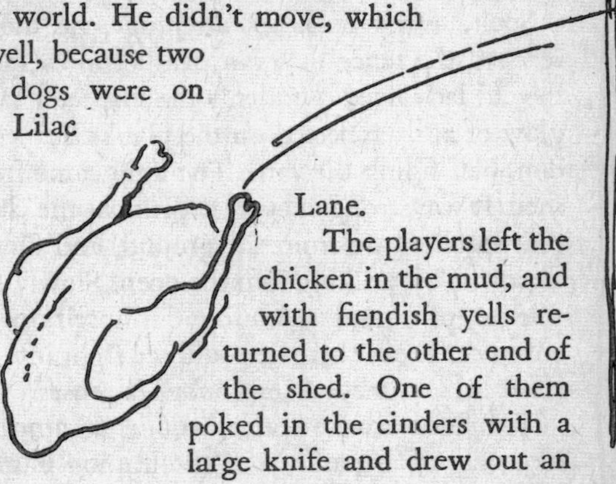

The players left the chicken in the mud, and with fiendish yells returned to the other end of the shed. One of them poked in the cinders with a large knife and drew out an

enormous potato burnt black by the fire. Cheers greeted its appearance and they all took off their masks to eat. It was only then that Sinet came out of his nightmare and recognized the ten children of Gaby's gang. He had seen enough for one evening, he decided, as he slid away behind the wood piles. Coming into the open too soon would only spoil things. What was important was that now he knew where to find the children at any given time.

Gaby was furious: he had let them take the masks away, but not the chicken.

'You're jolly well not going to pull the Billette Factory to bits,' he growled, as he chewed his share of the potato. 'What on earth would people say if they found us holding Mardi Gras the week before Christmas?'

'We could take just a little bit,' protested Zidore equally roused. 'There's surely no harm in that. Anyway, the damp's got into it all. No one would want to buy it.'

'I couldn't agree more,' answered Gaby. 'It just isn't worth it. If you go strutting around the streets all dressed up in masks and beards and the lot, it'll only attract attention. Anyway, from now on, no one's going to take a single thing away with him unless I say he can!'

'We haven't explored it all yet,' said Juan, his eyes glinting greedily. 'I bet there's a lot more interesting stuff at the other end of the factory.'

'We'll find out tomorrow,' said Gaby. 'But don't forget the candles. Everyone bring as many ends as possible so that we can see for an hour or two.'

Fernand was thinking as he stared at the little golden flames that flickered in the heart of the fire. While most of the gang regarded this business of the key as a heaven-sent gift and left it at that, he was anxious to get it straight. It was true that the key opened the doors of one of the deserted factories on the edge of Louvigny-Triage, which was gradually falling apart under the assault of wind and weather, but the too-brief light of Gaby's spluttering matches had shown them nothing very wonderful, apart from the shelves of carnival novelties in the stockroom. Yet from the moment when Tatave had collided with old Zigon's pram, the horse had led them from one adventure to another. And still there was no solution to the mystery.

'Tomorrow,' he whispered to Marion, 'we'll scour the place from top to bottom. We've got to find it.'

'Find what?' said Marion, shaking her tangled locks. 'You can keep the whole jolly factory and all this junk. What I want to find are the crooks that stole the horse.'

'Me too,' muttered Fernand. 'They both go together.'

Gaby gave orders for the next day. Masks and beards were all put away in the packing-case cupboard, and the 'club' was tidied up. Zidore for his part put the fire out and then the whole gang made off in complete silence along Lilac Lane.

Before they emerged into the rue de la Vache Noire, Gaby had a good look round. Not a soul was in sight.

'Even though it's dark,' he whispered to the others, 'it's best not to show ourselves too much round here.'

'We don't want to go to the other extreme either,' Marion said, nudging him.

First Tatave and Bonbon, then Berthe and Mélie, and finally Zidore, Juan, and Criquet, slipped up the road at intervals of a few seconds and vanished under Marion's watchful eyes in the direction of the rue des Petits-Pauvres. Gaby was watching the bottom of the street towards the main road, and Fernand the misty open spaces of the Clos Pecqueux, on which white patches of snow glittered here and there. But nothing moved and they saw no one. Marion rubbed noses with her dogs, gave them each a lump of sugar, and sent them home. Before they separated, the three elder children gave each other a warm hand-clasp.

'Good,' said Gaby. 'I'm off home. See you others tomorrow.'

'Don't run into Roublot,' called Fernand with a laugh.

Gaby had the key of the Billette Factory on him, the key that the horse without a head had brought up the night his belly had been emptied. They had each agreed to take it in turns to guard the key, thus giving their enemies less chance of getting it. The key itself was nothing: one good blow from a crowbar would have been enough to break down the door it locked. But Gaby, Marion, and Fernand had the feeling that its label of yellowed wood carried an address that a bunch of ugly customers would be only too glad to know. It was good fun to keep them guessing.

Three nights running the ten made their way to the factory without giving themselves the least cause for anxiety. When they got to the bottom of the rue des Petits-Pauvres they climbed under the barbed-wire and dashed off towards the Black Cow standing out tall and black on the sky-line. No one would have seen anything odd about their high-spirited charge, and Gaby took good care that the gang kept no sort of order, so as to give no sign that they had a fixed objective before them. In any case, the misty weather helped them to guard their secret, for from about four o'clock the haze from Louvigny-Cambrouse was thick enough to hide the last lap of their journey from the neighbours' eyes. The ten regrouped behind the bulk of the old engine and then set straight off at a good pace towards the corner of César Aravant's goods-yard.

The spot was always deserted; the only movement came from the trains that whistled loudly as they approached Le Triage. A dirt road between two sheds gave right on to the Ponceau road, dominated in its turn by the railway embankment. Gaby took up his post at the corner of the wall, one eye fixed on the black hole that was the mouth of the tunnel, out of which would jolt the occasional car or the odd railwayman on his way home to Louvigny. Once all was clear, Gaby sent his companions across two by two, telling them to hug the embankment. A hundred yards farther on, the saw-tooth roofs of the Billette Factory rose above its dingy concrete front. The first to arrive just opened the heavy doors and, slipping through the crack, awaited the others. When they were all there Gaby closed the gates and turned the key in the lock. They could then go where they pleased without fear of interruption.

The workshops had been abandoned at the height of their activity and the papier-mâché and collodion vats were still half-full of a dried-up pulp, the benches were thick with many-coloured ribbons, gilt paper, and the moulds for the masks that grinned down from the walls, while the paint-spattered floors were covered with a flood of spangles and paper streamers. For some reason or other, the carnival-accessories trade had fallen on a lean year before the war, and this factory had never recovered. However, the wreckage didn't seem to cast the slightest gloom on the spirits of the children from the rue des Petits-Pauvres.

Gaby wandered round, a pig's head on his shoulders, and two cardboard pistols in his hands. On turning a corner of the passage, he was not in the least surprised to run into a lion on its hind legs with a paper ruff round its neck.

'Who are you?' he asked the lion.

'Mélie!' mewed the lion in a strangled little voice.

Fernand suddenly bumped into a fairy in a black domino with a tall, pointed hat crowned by a star, waving a sausage instead of a magic wand.

'Marion!' he laughed. 'Your eyes give you away!'

Tatave only tried the gazookas – piles of them – and when he had found one to his liking he would lean his elbows on a bench, blow out his fat cheeks, and treat his friends to a monotonous little tune. Every so often the whine of the music was drowned in the roar of a passing train. The thin walls trembled, but as the thunder of the express died away towards Melun or Louvigny, in the silence Tatave's husky fluting could be heard again, an accompaniment to the witches' sabbath that the children were kicking up in workshop after workshop.

Every ten minutes Criquet Lariqué would shout a demand to be installed member of the Grand Order of the Green Flimflam, First Class. Standing to attention before his peers, he would have a ribbon of crinkled paper, from which hung a huge lead star, put round his neck by Juan. The three girls would kiss the new knight on each cheek and Zidore would slap each shoulder with the flat of a sword. But the ritual was not complete without one last gesture. At the word of command Criquet would make a smart right turn, and bow submissively, whereupon Gaby ceremoniously kicked him in the pants, to the applause of the crowd!

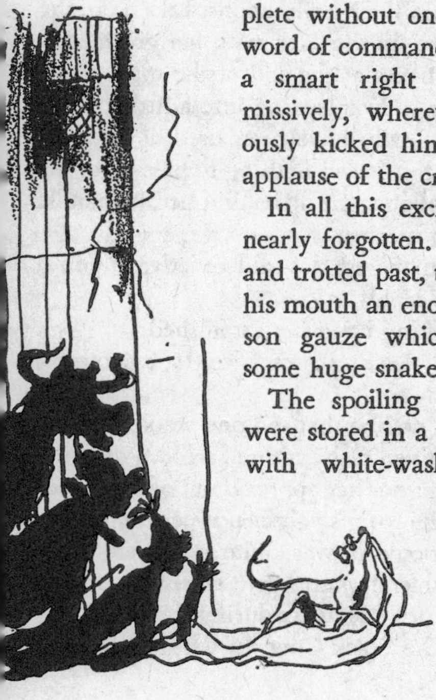

In all this excitement the horse was nearly forgotten. Fifi joined in the fun and trotted past, tail in air, trailing from his mouth an enormous length of crimson gauze which followed him like some huge snake.

The spoiling stocks of the factory were stored in a vast, windowless room with white-washed walls, separated from the workshops by a wire grill. No one ventured there without Gaby, who thus tried to limit the pillage and prevent any one's stupidity and carelessness sending the whole place up in flames. For three days running they explored the building with unabating excitement. By the flickering light of a candle the older ones methodically went through every cupboard, every shelf, and all the piles of boxes neatly stacked against the partitions that divided the various rooms. There was every sort of thing there, from the most grotesque of masks to the most ridiculous of carnival properties, such as the squeakers which Zidore would blow into your face from six feet away, or a fat cigar which would blossom into a bunch of paper flowers when Berthe Gédéon puffed at it.

Marion led the way in their explorations. Like a cat, she seemed to be able to see in the dark with her green eyes. Moving some of the boxes at the end of the main storeroom, she came across a door leading into a little cubbyroom, she came across a door leading into a little cubby-hole which must originally have been used as a cloakroom. She tiptoed in, but found nothing to pass on to the others. By chance Bonbon came up behind her, his candle held aloft. She caught his arm.

'You mustn't go in there,' she said quietly, but in a voice that brooked no reply.

'No?' he asked, looking up at her astonished.

'No!' she repeated, leading him back to the others. 'And don't ask me why not.'

When Marion said no like that, no one would ever go against her decision. Even Gaby himself seldom did anything without watching for her approval out of the corner of his eye. She was the gang's conscience personified.

When they went home it was quite dark, and they stumbled in the bomb-craters that five or six Allied air-raids had left in the Clos Pecqueux during the war. They had to pass close by the Black Cow. In the darkness she had the air of some monster crouched ready to pounce on them, and though she no longer scared the older children, the younger ones were only too glad to hurry past.

'Don't go so fast,' Gaby shouted to them – then, with a guffaw, 'She won't bite you!'

Whereupon a volley of stones clanged against the old engine. There was a great hole in one side of the boiler, and you could easily scramble inside if you hauled yourself up by the front buffers. In broad daylight there was nothing to it, and many a time had one or other of the ten ripped a skirt or torn the seat out of a pair of trousers in hiding inside the Cow. But at night it was a different matter, and not even the boldest would have put foot inside for worlds.

The evening before, as the gang came up to the threatening mass of rusty metal, Zidore had thrown out a challenge that no one had taken up as yet.

'I'll give my share of potatoes to whoever goes inside the boiler!' he shouted to the others.

Tatave, Gaby, and Juan had laughed loudly, but had been careful not to commit themselves.

And now they reached the Cow.

'Hey!' said Marion of a sudden – she was walking a little behind the main body – 'light me a candle, somebody! I want to make sure there's no one inside.'

'Don't be silly!' answered Gaby. 'Zidore was only joking.'

'Give me a hand,' said Marion, who had now made up her mind.

Tatave gave her a leg up, and she scrambled on to the buffers. Then they saw her edge her way along the huge boiler, shading the candle against the wind with one hand. The hole was at the other end, about ten feet forward of the driver's cab.

First the candle and then her head and shoulders vanished inside. Dirty water, in which writhed a few bits of broken tube, covered the bottom of the boiler. Marion held up her candle and looked towards the twisted bars and cast-iron plates that were all that was left of the fire-box. Nothing there. Then she turned her head to look at the other end.

'Well?' shouted the others outside.

Marion blew out her candle and drew back, tight-lipped.

'Not a thing!' she called down cheerfully. 'And not a soul; I must have been imagining things!'

She leapt to the ground, and, pulling a lump of old iron out of the grass, hurled it with all her might at the tall engine cowl.

'Boom!' bellowed the Black Cow in the middle of the Clos Pecqueux.

Soon they could see the sunken road whose distantly spaced gas-lamps shed their flickering light, and then the narrow gully that was the rue des Petits-Pauvres and the dark mass of the town beyond. Gaby called a short halt before they got through the barbed wire, to give Marion time to whistle up Fanfan and Butor from the other side of the main road. Once she was back with her two hounds they crossed the road and fled down Lilac Lane.

They felt really at home in the Club after all the exciting hours they had spent in their treasure-house, the Billette Factory. The fire caught and was soon blazing, and the girls set to, brewing the soup and spreading melted chocolate on slices of toast. Meanwhile Gaby took stock of the situation and collected his companions' reports.

The most important news came from Juan and the darky who lived among the riff-raff of the slums.

'Last night,' said the Spaniard, 'a truck went up and down the Ponceau road three or four times between the station and the Faubourg-Bacchus. It was moving very slowly and the driver seemed to be looking for something. There may be nothing to it, because we work the other side of the station . . .'

'What sort of truck was it?' Gaby cut in.

'Grey Renault, with a hood,' said Criquet.

'It was a grey-green one the other night,' said Fernand.

'There were a couple of fellows beside the driver,' Juan went on. 'That's what caught our eye.'

'You didn't see who they were?'

'Couldn't: it was far too dark!'

Then Fernand took up his tale. 'Well, I've a feeling that Sinet and Lamy are hanging round us. As I was going home last night, I saw the two of them sneaking off down the rue des Alliés.'

'They'd do a jolly sight better if they'd look for the horse,' said Zidore bitterly 'I'd jolly well like to know what the pair of smart alicks have done to get it back.'

Marion looked up. 'Perhaps,' she said quietly, 'they're guarding us without our realizing it. Because those two cops are around, the crooks haven't dared to come too near us. If we hadn't told the police, they'd have been after us long ago, and they wouldn't have been very nice about it either.'

'What makes you think that?' asked Gaby, surprised.

Marion pushed a few bits of wood into the fire with the end of her toe.

'Just a moment ago,' she said, 'there were two men inside the Cow!'

All around her, jaws stopped munching.

'Two men!' cried Gaby. 'Why on earth didn't you tell me right away?'

'Well, there was no need to scare you,' Marion replied. 'Anyway, it was much better to let them think we hadn't spotted them! I couldn't see very well, the wind was blowing the candle about the whole time, but I did catch sight of them. They were crouched in one end like a pair of sardines, pressed against the sides of the boiler.'

This was news. They all stopped eating.

'It wouldn't be wise to use the old route to the factory after that,' Gaby declared. 'What do you think? They may have been watching to see which way we went.'

'If they were around they wouldn't wait until it was dark to do that,' said Fernand.

'They're running a big risk showing their faces in the neighbourhood,' added Juan. 'They must have been hanging about the Clos Pecqueux. When they heard us coming round the goods-yard they must have got scared, and hidden in the boiler.'

'They'll be there tomorrow night again for sure,' said Marion. 'But we've nothing to worry about. Our way across the fields is still the safest. The Ponceau road's so narrow, and you never know who's going to pop out of the tunnel. It's much the best to cut across the Clos Pecqueux. We know it like the back of our hands, and we can scatter easily.'

Berthe and Mélie, Criquet and Bonbon listened to it all with growing delight and excitement, as though they were being told the special rules of a new sort of hide-and-seek, with the treasures of the Billette Factory thrown in for good measure. The bigger ones treated it more seriously, it is true, but even they did not see the danger of what it really was. They felt that it was just a matter of drawing the crooks into a well-laid trap, and Marion thought they had already taken the bait. No one knew what had become of the horse, and it seemed most unlikely that they would ever again see it tearing down the rue des Petits-Pauvres on its three wheels. This being so, the ten were determined that someone should pay dearly for it, and they were not very particular who that someone was

They had to wait a good while at the end of Lilac Lane. Footsteps were coming up the rue de la Vache Noire; there was a murmur of voices; they stopped and then went on more slowly and softly – they were not those of innocent passers-by.

Gaby was worried about his friends, and decided to accompany the whole group as far as the cross-roads at the rue Cécile.

Marion slipped off on her own towards the low-roofed cottages of Louvigny-Cambrouse that shut off the country-side beyond the main road. It was the time she generally made this round – so as not to disturb anyone. She set off at a good pace along the muddy tracks that led across the fields from the road, went boldly into back-yards, through hedges, clung to garden railings, and her shrill whistle was like the humming of a song which the howl of the wind through the bare branches could not drown.

That night the dogs in Louvigny-Cambrouse seemed very restless; but without bursting out into the bark they gave when they saw a cat or someone trying to sneak some vegetables out of the garden. Housewives got anxious and peered through windows.

'The dog's growling,' they would say. 'I'd better have a look outside.'

'Don't worry,' their husbands would reply, puffing at their pipes; 'it's only the girl with the dogs going her round.'

Marion went as far as the fine houses in the Quartier-Neuf, and finished her walk passing by the workers' tenements in Petit-Louvigny. Juan heard her whistle and came to the door.

'What are you up to round here?'

'Look,' she answered, showing him her sopping coat and mud-caked shins. 'I've done my round, and now I'm going home.'

'How are they?' asked Juan, who thought of her dogs as human beings.

'They're all right,' Marion answered, with an odd sort of smile. 'I bet they give us something to laugh over before very long.'

'Who's got the key?' went on Juan. Talk of the dogs sent his mind to the horse.

'It's Zidore's turn tonight,' answered Marion.

'I hope he won't leave it behind at home.'

'Not likely. He sleeps with it under his pillow.'

CHAPTER 6

All the Dogs in the World

SATURDAY isn't much of a day for school-children in Louvigny. Most of them see their father start a lazy morning, look in the local paper to find what's on at the cinema, or set out on his motor-bike, fishing-tackle strapped on the back. Meanwhile they themselves go through a regular third degree in a dingy building in the rue Poit from a gentleman in spectacles, who grills them about the Pass of Thermopylae and the murder of the Duc de Guise.

That morning, and again in the afternoon, Monsieur Juste, the schoolmaster, noticed how preoccupied the older boys – Gaby, Fernand, and Zidore – were, and guessed from experience that they had a lot planned.

Next door Madame Juste was not surprised to find Marion was absent. It was true that this happened quite often; the child was either helping her poor mother or somebody else. In the infants' class, young Mademoiselle Berry suddenly burst out laughing and then made Bonbon stand in the corner for ten minutes, to teach him not to wear a great bulbous red false nose in form. The nose was confiscated until the end of the period, which was fortunately not long in coming.

None of the gang went

home after school. Madame Lariqué, Madame Babin, and Madame Gédéon would have been able to keep their offspring indoors by saying what dreadful weather it had been all day, and that wouldn't have suited Gaby in the very least. He wanted to have every single member of the gang to hand. It wasn't snowing much; every now and then one gust of wind would bring a handful of flakes to dance at the end of the street, until a moment later another gust would come and scatter them. But already it was getting very dark and their knees were blue with the bitter cold.

Marion was waiting for the gang at the corner of the rue des Petis-Pauvres. She made them all come home with her to leave their satchels there and have a good cup of steaming hot chocolate. Little Bonbon had put on his false nose again, and was brandishing his enormous revolver most threateningly.

'You might just as well have left that old thing at home, for all the good it did you last time,' said Zidore, laughing.

'I know it can't kill anyone,' agreed Bonbon regretfully, 'but I don't feel so frightened when I'm holding it.'

The first thing Gaby did was to check on what they had for lighting. In all, there were five candle-ends and two boxes of matches, and he divided them among the elder children.

While the younger ones were being wrapped up in their scarves, Madame Fabert came in. She took these brigands' visit very well, considering that she found they had eaten up her supply of bread for the week-end during the five minutes they had been there. Marion was always truthful, and smiling at her mother she said:

'We're just going to have a run round the Clos to get warmed up.'

Madame Fabert shrugged her shoulders resignedly. 'Well, off you go, then,' she said, 'but take care you don't fall down and hurt yourselves in those bomb-craters. I think I'd rather have you going at sixty miles an hour on that wretched horse of yours.'

The ten crossed the road together and slipped under the barbed wire without any attempt at concealment. The Clos Pecqueux stretched in front of them until it was lost in the evening mist, as quiet and deserted as on the previous evenings.

Gaby, Fernand, and Zidore boldly led the way, each swinging a good thick cudgel picked from Madame Fabert's wood-pile. Juan hugged the long knife they used for the potatoes to his chest, while Tatave brandished an elegant poker with a copper handle. Bonbon came next, shooting with his heavy revolver at the crows in the distance.

'Take aim! Fire! Bang! He's dead!' cried Bonbon, closing his left eye.

But the crow would flap off cawing his denial.

Marion brought up the rear, alone, her hands thrust deep into the pockets of her jacket. A smile played round her lips and it was not one of complete kindness.

They reached the middle of the Clos. Gaby went straight on without stepping a yard out of his course. Instinctively they stopped talking, and the younger ones kept close to their elders. A little fresh snow had caught in the cracks and crannies of the Black Cow and lay along the top of her rusty boiler. As they went past they hurled the usual rain of stones against her and set her booming like the great bell of a cathedral. Then the ten trotted away to the fence round César Aravant's goods-yard. They reached the alley, and Marion let the others file past, while, pressing close to the wall, she watched the empty spaces of the Clos Pecqueux.

A moment later two indistinct figures came out of the Black Cow. One of them hurried back towards the houses of Louvigny, while the other followed the tracks of the gang, taking care not to be seen and stopping now and then to get the lie of the deserted buildings.

Quickly Marion left her observation post and caught up with her friends in the Ponceau road. She said nothing, for one still couldn't tell what was going to happen. She contented herself with tipping the wink to Gaby to set him on his guard. Whereupon he opened the gate, let them all in and then carefully shut and double-locked it. It was so dark that they had to light their candles immediately to see their way into the workshop.

Gaby stayed outside a moment to have a brief word with Marion and Fernand. 'The main gate won't hold ten seconds with men who've got the tools they have,' he said anxiously. 'The wood's all rotten round the lock.'

'That doesn't matter a bit,' said Marion. 'You just barricade yourselves in the store-room and lock the three communicating doors behind you. They'll lose a good ten minutes breaking through, and there's a lot you can do in ten minutes. The main thing is to get them inside and keep them there. I'll do the rest.'

Fernand nodded.

'I'll go straight up and keep a look out of the little round window above the gate.'

He tiptoed up to the door and climbed the narow staircase leading to the two empty rooms on the floor above. Half-way up was a skylight. Slowly he poked his head out and looked up and down the Ponceau road.

Complete darkness had fallen on the Clos Pecqueux. Yellow lights glowed in the nearest houses in Louvigny.

The road was quite dark, in spite of the glaring lights above the railway lines. Fernand listened in vain. Every sound in the neighbourhood was drowned by the hissing of the shunting engines and the roar of the trains passing through. Sticking his head out still farther, he looked towards Louvigny. The harsh glare of a pair of headlights lit up the sunken road, and as they came sweeping nearer and nearer they flashed for a second on the faces of the neighbouring buildings. Instead of turning and going through the tunnel, the car kept straight on, and pulled up in front of the fence across the end of the road. The headlights were switched off and Fernand heard the doors bang.

'Can you see anything?' a voice behind him asked. 'Let me have a look.'

Marion had crept up. Gently she pushed him aside and poked her head through the opening. At that moment another car came from Louvigny; its headlights swept across the skyline, catching the girl's face in their glare.

'Look out,' whispered Fernand. 'They'll see you!'

As before, the car came through the tunnel, pulled up in the darkness by the goods-yard, and switched off its lights.

'It's them all right!' whispered Marion.

Then without a word she pointed to something outside oposite the skylight.

A passenger train was slowing down to take the Louvigny curve, and its lights flickered confusedly across the ground below them. Fernand looked: on the other side of the road a man was waiting, leaning up against the retaining wall of the embankment. He was so close that it took Fernand's breath away. The man switched on a torch and flashed it off and on to call up the others. Then he ran the beam over the factory walls.

The two children listened. There was a crunch of

gravel below the window. Fernand leant still further out and suddenly spotted five dark figures moving along beside the wall in single file.

'They're inside,' muttered a voice. 'You can see a light moving in the other end of the building.'

Noiselessly Fernand and Marion climbed down and took up their position in the entrance hall. There was a dull rumbling in the distance, gradually growing louder and louder until it set every window in the building rattling. The Melun express hurtled past along the embankment beside the Ponceau road. The very ground trembled, then the thunder of its wheels grew less and less and slowly faded away.

'Warn the others,' said Marion, 'and don't bother about me. Barricade yourselves in the end room as strongly as you can; you must hold out as long as possible.'

'What are you going to do?'

'I'll get out through the little yard at the back and cut across the fields. I shan't have long – but don't worry, I'll be back.'

She disappeared among the shadows in the passage. The door gave another crack: a ray of light filtered through the broken panels, which were being violently shaken from outside.

'Come on, give her a shove!' someone shouted.

Fernand turned and ran into the first workshop. Gaby joined him, his face showing his alarm, his hand clutching a candle-end.

'Well?'

'They're here!' panted Fernand. 'We've just got time to bar the doors.

There was no key in the first one in the hall, so they dragged the work-benches across the opening and pushed them flush against the iron of the door.

There was a dull crash from the direction of the road. Both leaves of the door had given way under the pressure of the besiegers. Gaby and Fernand dashed into the next workshop. A communicating door, its upper panel of glass, separated this room from the other. It locked, however.

'It won't take them long to smash their way through this,' shrugged Gaby.

'They'll waste two or three minutes,' answered Fernand, 'and Marion says we must gain time.'

The younger ones were calmly trying on wigs and false beards in the store-room at the end, standing round Zidore, who was dressed up as a demon; Tatave had already broken a dozen gazookas; Berthe and Mélie were hurling paper streamers furiously at each other; and Criquet decked out in a three-cornered hat, was having a row of medals pinned on his chest by General Bonbon Louvrier de Louvigny.

'Stop this fooling!' growled Gaby in an awful voice. 'The crooks who pinched our horse will be on top of us any minute now. Man the barricades, all of you! Come on, shift that pile of cardboard boxes over there in front of the door!'

The grill that separated the stock-room from the rest of the building was made of solid slats of wood that ran from floor to ceiling. The double door, strengthened with wooden cross beams, was fastened top and bottom by two thick bolts which could not be reached from outside. But it still wasn't enough to stop the intruders.

Without wasting a second they all fell to work, piling boxes of carnival novelties up against the partition, the heaviest at the bottom as a firm foundation for their barricade and the lighter ones tossed in showers on the top. As they fell some of them broke open and the place was soon festooned with a tangle of paper chains of all colours, plumes of horse-hair, chinese umbrellas, cardboard crowns, jack-in-the-boxes, streamers of artificial flowers, a snow of spangles, armfuls of gazookas and rattles, castanets, false beards, false noses, false teeth, and all the thousand and one treasures of this Ali Baba's cave of a store-room.

An appalling crash and the tinkle of broken glass came from the neighbouring room. A flash-light beam played furtively upon the bluish glass of the roof; heavy boots clumped across the concrete floor, and slowly drew near the store-room.

'One more door,' said Fernand, 'and then we'll see what these toy thieves really look like.'

'Out with the candles,' hissed Gaby, trembling with excitement. 'Get back to the far end of the store, behind the last pile of boxes. If anyone laughs I'll do them.'

Bottling their laughter the children tiptoed off, tripping over the oddments that littered the passage down the middle. From one end of the room to the other the cases of goods were carefully stacked head high, leaving a gap about a yard wide between each pile. These cardboard fortifications not only gave an illusion of safety, but as

Gaby said, could easily be pushed over if it came to a tussle, and so create the most glorious chaos.

The last door made the toughs sweat a bit. It was metal-sheathed and Gaby had securely double-locked it. They had to join forces to smash it in. They used a work-bench which they swung like a battering-ram, backwards and forwards, their curses setting the rhythm. All at once one of the panels gave way completely and most of the door-frame with it. The crash stifled the giggles of Berthe and Mélie, set off by the cascade of paper streamers that had fallen out of the half-open cupboard and buried them up to their necks.

Gaby and Fernand were side by side, entrenched behind the first wall of boxes. By pushing two of them out of the pile they had made themselves a narrow peep-hole. On the other side of the slatted partition they saw the toughs come into the room, one behind the other. The dancing light of a torch flashed on the burly forms and now caught one scowling face and now another. The one in the lead put his foot in the pig's head mask, which happened to be lying in his path. He tripped and measured his length on the floor, bringing down with him a pile of paint-cans in a glorious clatter. He spat and swore, and, cursing his comrades and puffing and blowing, he heaved himself to his feet. Quite by accident he got a long black beard stuck to the end of his nose. This mishap cheered Gaby's gang; the tension had been growing unbearable.

'You won't get anywhere until you get some decent light,' came a deep voice in the background. 'The fuse-box is out here in the entrance hall. Knock the front off and put in some fresh wires. No one will see us. The nearest house is a good half-mile away.'

Two minutes later a harsh light was playing from the

bulbs that ran the length of the roof upon the grand chaos the children's visits had made, and on the fading treasures of the factory. Satisfied, the crooks dashed forward to the partition. There were five of them. Fernand and Gaby had no difficulty in picking out Pépé and Ugly in their leather jackets, and a little behind them, as though rather unsure of himself, the tall shape of Roublot. The other two wore heavy overcoats, the collars turned up so that their faces could not be seen properly.

Roughly, Ugly rattled the slats, muttering under his breath.

'Those little blighters have locked themselves in behind here. Well, we'll soon shift 'em!'

He went for the door with a crow-bar. But the cross-beams were thick and the bolts were solid steel, and the door held firm. Red with anger, Ugly hurled his tool away, and poking his face through the slats he yelled: 'You in there! Get this door open, and make it snappy, or I'll wring your blasted necks!'

'Open up, you little ruffians!' added Pépé.

Nothing stirred in the store-room.

'That's not the way to talk to children,' said one of the men in overcoats, quietly. (He seemed to be the leader.) 'Here, let me.'

Then, pushing the two others aside, he looked inquisitively between the slats. A solitary bulb hung over the door and dimly lit the long store-room with its grey steel cupboards and regular walls of boxes across the room.

'Come, come, come, come, come!' he sang out, as though calling in the hens for feeding. 'Don't be naughty. Open the door like good children and no one will be cross. Here's a hundred francs for the first one to come out.'

There was not a sound from the store. No one wanted

the hundred francs, and Tatave for one would have willingly given a hundred thousand to be somewhere else. Zidore and Juan had just found a box of bangers in their 'wall.' These bangers were little round paper balls filled with sand and holding a detonator cap. A hard throw would send them off with a fine explosion. Taking a handful each, they jumped up and threw them over the top of the boxes. They made a terrific bang-bang as they went off against the partition. It was like a burst of tommy-gun fire. Taken by surprise, the men instinctively drew back, shielding their heads with their arms. At the same time Gaby and Fernand leapt back to rejoin their friends.

'Help yourselves!' Zidore whispered. 'But let's shift a bit, or they'll spot us!'

The five crooks, boiling with rage, once more returned to the partition, this time with pistols drawn.

'Well, if you like that sort of game,' the leader shouted at the children, 'we'll join in too!'

And sliding his hand between the slats, he blindly let loose a volley of shots. The force of the bullets hitting and rebounding off the cupboards opened their doors and poured their contents on to the children crouching below. The crash of the explosions only roused the children still more, and Berthe and Mélie grabbed their share of bangers. One after the other the two girls, Fernand and Gaby, Zidore and Juan, hurled their grenades against the partition. One moment they were on their feet and the next they were full length in the heaps of crêpe-paper that carpeted the floor.

Roublot and Ugly slipped out into the next-door workshop. They came back dragging the bench which they had used before as a battering-ram. All together the five of them picked up the heavy table and brought it crash-

BANGERS
GAMES
TRICKS
Home

ing against the door. The panels cracked and part of the barricade the children had made collapsed under the shock.

A real storm of bangers burst with a blinding flash against the partition. The second blow from the battering-ram tore the bolt out of the bottom of the door, smashed in the lower panel, and brought down a whole mound of boxes. All the children were now on their feet and, throwing caution to the winds, they hurled their bombs by the handful, harassing the five men as they drew back for their last assault.

'What can Marion be doing?' muttered Fernand as he scraped the last handful of bangers from the bottom of the box.

*

Marion jumped over the low wall at the end of the yard and landed as lightly as a cat on the other side. It was very dark by now, but a fresh fall of snow covered the ground and by its pale glitter you could make out the mounds and hollows in the ground, above all the dangerous bomb-craters that riddled the bottom of the field beside the railway tracks.

Marion took to her heels and dashed into the darkness, heading for the ghostly mass of the rusty old Black Cow faintly outlined by the lights of the town behind it.

The snow went on falling gently, but the wind had fallen away. The noise of the traffic died down towards Triage and gradually this little corner of the suburbs became as quiet as the country.

When she reached the old engine, Marion stopped to rest for a second. Then she put two fingers between her teeth, took a deep breath, and began to whistle. Her shrill, wavering call travelled across the Clos Pecqueux, making itself heard above the roar of the traffic on the main roads and penetrated the streets, the alleys, the back-yards, the gardens, the sheds, and the barns.

Turning towards the lights of Louvigny that shone in her face, Marion whistled with all her might, not weakening but rather gaining power from the echo from the

embankment, which prolonged the sinister note. Through the bitter night, she whistled up help for the children from the rue des Petits-Pauvres.

Butor and Fanfan, Marion's two farm dogs, were the first to hear her urgent summons. They were hunting a cat at the head of the rue de la Vache Noire. The hair on their backs rose and, leaving the big tom, they cleared the barbed wire at one bound and hurled themselves into the darkness of the Clos Pecqueux. At the foot of the rue des Petits-Pauvres, Marion's twelve patients snored on, and the alert Fifi was the only one to jump the fence and run like a hare towards the Black Cow.

Close on her heels came the three aristocrats of the rue Cécile – Hugo, Fritz, and César. Shoulder to shoulder they took the corner of the cross-roads and vanished as fast as they had come.

Dingo, Cobbler Gally's old spaniel, got under way more slowly, crossed the road behind them, and slipped under the barbed wire with an angry growl. One after the other, Pipotte, old Monsieur Gédéon's bitch, and Moko, the fox-terrier belonging to the Babin family, came down the rue des Petits-Pauvres, and after them five ugly mongrels from Cité Ferrand: Mataf, Doré, Jeremie,

Ursule, and Drinette. The whole mob of them turned the corner at full speed, heads down, never a bark, and nearly knocked down the solitary pedestrian who was coming up the Ponceau road. Mustafa, the one-eyed Alsatian from the Bar de l'Auvergnat, and Zanzi, Madame Louvrier's poodle, came galloping along with Emile and Fido, the two retrievers owned by Monsieur Manteau, the Mayor of Louvigny. And those four nobly swelled the muster.

All the while Marion whistled.

Gamin, Monsieur Joye's black-and-white terrier, soon turned the

corner of the rue Aubertin and raced up the rue de la Vache Noire slightly ahead of the reinforcements from Louvigny-Cambrouse. The latter came helter-skelter across the main road, not bothering about the glaring headlights or the screeching brakes.

Mignon, the bulldog belonging to Maubert the small-holder, brought with him the rough-and-tough mongrels from the neighbourhood of les Maches: Filon, Canard, Betasse, Flip, and Briquet. And behind them came the farm dogs from the Bas-Louvigny, dark, shaggy, snarling, snapping brutes: Raleur, and Nougat, limping Croquant (though he didn't limp now) and yellow-eyed Charlot – scarred, and with most of his ears chewed off – Taquin, a mangy beast, and Canon the chicken-thief. This robber band came pattering along the tarmac of the main road. It was a wonderful sight to see the entire dog population of Louvigny in migration from one side of the town to the other.

And it was even better to see the toffs of the Quartier-Neuf joining in the game and sending such clipped and combed champions as Otto de la Ville-Neuberg du Pacq des Primevères, the boxer whose pedigree covered four whole pages, and whose daily dish was a pound of the best-quality minced beef; Bébé, the black Schnauzer with eyes like a goat; Hubert, the boar-hound, four times a medal winner, who could jump any wall; Popoff, the greyhound, once famous in the stadium; Zoum, the griffon, with an insatiable appetite for slippers and soft furnishings; and then five little dogs of all shapes and sizes, all a little over-plump, and all highly scented. Every one of them had passed through Marion's hand for some cure or other. Yes, the toffs of the Quartier-Neuf were hastening eagerly to the rallying place.

And still Marion went on whistling in the darkness of

the Clos Pecqueux. A faint echo even reached the little houses of Petit Louvigny and the Faubourg-Bacchus, and all at once every dog in the place seemed to go mad: rag-pickers' mongrels for the most part, good for nothing and living like outlaws on the fringes of the shopping streets. Leaving whatever they were doing, the rag-tag and bob-tail came out of the wooden huts and the waste land, entered the town-centre, crossed the Grand'rue and the rue Piot, turned up the rue des Alliés, and dashed full-cry down the rue des Petits-Pauvres, quite blocking the pavement. Pipi, Juan's lemon-and-white fox-terrier, was leading the pack with old Chable's dog, Arthur, a short-legged mongrel with a jackal's head, a coat as rough as a bass-broom, and one eye black and one eye blue. Then came Caillette, Frisé, Loupiotte l'Apache, Chopine, old Zigon's bitch, Golo, the Lariqués' lurcher, the old pug Adolf, Polyte, Bidasse, Gros-Père, and a dozen other flea-ridden curs, who changed name and home regularly once a week.

Planted beneath the threatening bulk of the Black Cow, Marion was still whistling as hard as she could when the first dogs reached her. She had half seen them in the darkness of Clos Pecqueux, wave upon wave of them, racing silently towards her. Not one of them gave tongue – Marion didn't allow that – and their feet pattered on the ground like a rain-storm. In a few seconds she found herself hemmed in by a growling mass that eagerly twisted and turned to touch her friendly hand or sniff her coat. The more dogs there were about her, the gentler and more caressing her whistle grew. Louvigny-Cambrouse and the Quartier-Neuf arrived almost together, and then came the flea-bitten rabble from the Faubourg-Bacchus.

Every so often the beam of a distant headlight caught

the group, and hundreds of eyes gleamed red and green around her, like so many fire-flies. The dogs whimpered with delight, and occasionally one or the other of them would give a plaintive little whine.

'Whisht!' said Marion, throwing wide here arms, 'here, here!'

The dogs closed round her, leaping, gazing adoringly up at her. Marion held out her arms, recognizing them by touch, stroking noses, patting backs, and calling them by name as she did so.

Then with a sharp call of 'Come!' she broke through them and set off running towards the bottom of the Clos Pecqueux. Obediently the dogs panted after her. The whole pack threaded their way through the narrow lane that led into the Ponceau road. As the dogs eagerly crowded after Marion, an express thundered along the embankment in a shimmer of golden lights.

Her pace slackened when she approached the factory. The splintered gates yawned black, but there was a glow of light above the workshop roof. From the depths of the building came a series of muffled thuds. She went in – or rather, she was pushed in by the wild rush of the dogs, who hurled themselves panting from room to room.

A cloud of acrid smoke hung about the end workshop. The partition was still holding – but only just. The five crooks were swinging their battering-ram for the final blow. With a crash, one half of the door fell in and brought down with it the barricade of boxes.

'Hey!' called Marion.

The astonished men turned, and their hands hung useless and their jaws dropped to see the girl and her sixty silent, straining hounds standing behind them. The dogs were waiting as though they were held back only by some invisible leash.

'Go on!' cried Marion in a shrill voice. 'Catch 'em! Pull 'em down! Rotten swine who pinch kids' toys in the rue des Petits-Pauvres!'

With a joyful bound the dogs fell to work.

CHAPTER 7

A Hundred Million Francs

AT SIX o'clock Monsieur Douin's relief signalman, his friend Gédéon, came on duty, and a few minutes later he himself left Box No. 118. Just at the moment there was a gap in the rail traffic through Le Triage, and thanks to this brief pause Monsieur Douin was able to hear, to his surprise, a series of shots, cries, and the sounds of a struggle coming from somewhere beside the tracks, or, more exactly, from the sinister Clos Pecqueux. Turning his head, he at once spotted the bluish light reflected through the glass roof of the Billette Factory. This was something quite out of the ordinary. He had never seen a soul set foot in that islet of condemned buildings for the last fifteen years at least. Monsieur Douin then turned on his heel and climbed back into the signal-box. He picked up the telephone and warned the station-master's office that there appeared to be a gang battle taking place in one of the abandoned factories along the Ponceau road.

At that moment the two inspectors, Sinet and Lamy, were happily toasting their feet on the radiator in their office. The latter had just succeeded in persuading the former that it was the sheerest idiocy to go on his usual round of the saw-mill on such a bitter night, when Superintendent Blanchon burst in.

'Know the Billette Factory, 224 Ponceau road, carnival accessories of all kinds, masks, wigs, artificial flowers, paper decorations for parties and dances?' the grim-faced veteran asked them, all in one breath.

121

'No,' answered the two obstinately, as much as to say: 'And we don't want to, either!'

'Right! Take six men and the truck and have a look-see what's going on down there. I've just been warned there's a fight. Get a move on. I'll be in my office when you get back.'

Inspector Sinet swore under his breath. For three days the children had been as good as telling him about this. It was not for nothing that they'd been dressed up for Christmas as though it were Mardi Gras. And if they were involved, it would bring them back to that darned business of the horse, though Monsieur Blanchon didn't want to hear another word about that.

A few minutes later the Black Maria was tearing past the station and roaring down the Ponceau road, its siren screaming. It slowed down through the tunnel and pulled up sharply in front of the fence across the road. Two trucks were already parked, without lights, beside the wall round César Aravant's yard. Sinet recognized one of them immediately.

'Roublot's there,' he whispered to Lamy. 'It'll give me the greatest pleasure to put him under arrest!'

The eight men tumbled over the fence, and with Sergeant Tassart, who knew the place, at their head, they hurried along the muddy road. Two lighted windows stood out clearly in the general blackness. As he approached, Sinet heard a cry. He started to run, and soon the others were pounding along hard on his heels.

The door was open. Sinet drew his revolver and, crouching, plunged down the workshop under the centre lights. From the far end came a tremendous din of shouts and barks.

Suddenly, through the gun-smoke, he saw the wrecked store-room in the dim light. And then his eye fell on

Marion, Madame Fabert's little girl, inquisitively watching one corner of the room. Sinet turned and looked too. There in the corner, twisting and turning, growling and snapping in the half-light, was a pack of panting, angry, excited dogs: so that was where the barking was coming from! Right at the end, behind the shattered partition, were Gaby and the rest of the gang. They were jumping about like jack-in-the-boxes amid a mass of brightly coloured rubbish, shouldering their way through the stacks of cardboard boxes, knocking them down and spilling the contents, dragging paper streamers, hurling confetti, and tearing the paper to tatters when it caught round their legs.

Marion turned round sharply. She didn't seem in the least surprised to find that the police had arrived.

'There they are,' was all she said to Sinet, and pointed to the battling hounds.

'Who?' yelled Sinet, quite at sea.

'The thieves,' said Marion with a broad grin. 'The ones that pinched the horse.'

Whereupon, putting two fingers to her lips, she whistled shrilly.

It seemed to have the same effect on the dogs as a whiplash. They leaped aside, obediently came to heel round her, their heads raised, and their wild eyes flashing.

'Whisht!' said Marion.

She stretched out her arms, gently urged the dogs to the other end of the building, and drove them into a corner. It was just as well she did so, for in their state they would have been quite happy to go for a couple of policemen.

'I've got them now,' she said to Sinet. 'You won't have any trouble in picking up your thieves: they've had their lot.'

The policemen found the five men huddled against the

wall, their shoulders hunched, their clothes in ribbons, and in such a state that they had to haul them to their feet. Sinet retrieved four good pistols; they hadn't been much use, for the children and the dogs were in fine fettle.

While those five rogues were being handcuffed, Sinet turned his attention to Gaby.

'You've been up to some games!' he cried, pointing to the ravaged store-room and the shattered doors.

'No, we haven't,' retorted Gaby, red with anger. 'It was those swine! Potting at us through the slats!'

'How did you get into the factory?'

'We had a key, of course. They didn't have one, though! I say, there must be something pretty important for them to follow us right in here like that!'

But all the Inspector could get out of his prisoners was a string of oaths and a few plaintive groans. He went into the store, kicking a path as best he could through the litter of rubbish on the floor. Mélie, Babin and Tatave had hidden themselves as far back as they could get and they were now feverishly hunting among the last pile of boxes.

'We can't find Bonbon!' they called to the others. 'Come and help us!'

Rather anxiously, Sinet hurried over to lend them a hand. All the children except Marion, who kept an eye on her pack, joined him, laughing and pushing each other. Gaby, Fernand, Juan, and Zidore seemed to go quite mad as they leaped from pile to pile of broken boxes, putting the finishing touches to the sack of the Billette Factory. The Inspector's foot chanced to kick open a cardboard box. There, as though it were his coffin, lay a fair-haired, chubby infant, one arm raised, a huge revolver pointing straight at Sinet.

'One move and you're a dead duck!' said Bonbon, closing one eye.

Sinet just bent down, pulled him out by one leg, and sent him hopping off to join his elders.

'Empty the cupboards,' he ordered them. 'Chuck all this junk out. We must find ...'

'What?' cut in the grumbling voice of Gaby. 'Something big? Something small?'

'That depends,' was the vague reply. 'Anyway, it'll be something that'll stick out a mile in all this muck. Get looking!'

The children set to with a will.

In searching the other corner, Sinet discovered the door into the poky little room that Marion had forbidden to the younger children. No light from the store-room reached it. He switched on his torch and stepped inside. The beam swung round to show him metal coat-pegs, a row of dusty wash-basins, and a little barred window that looked out on to the yard.

Sinet went in farther and then felt his heels sink into something soft and springy which covered the floor in that spot. He nearly fell, and grabbed a cupboard to steady himself. In so doing his torch swept in a wide circle across the floor.

'Aha!' cried Inspector Sinet.

His bellow brought Lamy, two policemen, and all the children running. There was the Inspector, standing in the middle of the room with his mouth agape and his arms dangling at his sides, up to his ankles in a carpet of banknotes that shimmered in the flickering light of the torches.

Beside him stood a cupboard, both doors wide open, from which the wads of notes dropped gently down, to pile up softly round his feet. They fell from a big grey sack balanced on top of a pile of other sacks that filled the cupboard. When it was empty it fell with a plop to the ground.

Lamy counted the other sacks: there were eleven.

'I don't believe it,' gasped Sinet.

'Neither do I,' said Lamy, unsealing the topmost sack with his penknife.

A fresh cascade of wads tumbled out on to the ground with a silky rustle. Some of them burst with the fall, and the lovely new bank-notes fanned gently out. The two policemen just stared at each other.

'The hundred million francs from the Paris–Ventimiglia express,' murmured Sinet, in the seventh heaven of delight.

He turned and suddenly noticed the children's astonished faces peering round the edge of the door.

'Come here,' he said to Gaby.

The boy hurried forward, never sparing a glance at the fortune he was trampling under his hobnails. The Inspector grabbed him by the shoulders and shaking him roughly, shouted in his face.

'So you've been roaming round the building for the last three days, and not one of you had the least idea of coming into this room? You've never seen these bank-notes before, have you?'

'Of course we've seen them,' Gaby replied calmly. 'So what?'

'So what?' yelled the Inspector. 'And you've never thought to tell me, I suppose?'

Bewildered, Gaby turned to his friends as though asking their aid. Marion stepped forward.

'But, Inspector,' she said, 'there's so much of it! We thought it was false, like all the rest.'

The simplicity of the statement disarmed the Inspector. He let Gaby go and stood there, unable to think what to say next.

'Well, what are we going to do with these notes?' Lamy asked him.

'Get three of the men to help you carry the full sacks to the wagon,' answered Sinet. 'The kids will pick up all the ones on the floor and fill the empty sacks. I'll stay and keep an eye on them.'

From the eldest to the youngest they set to work right away. Gaby was furious, and picked up masses of the paper in his arms and stuffed it into the sacks with powerful blows of his fists.

'Thieves? Us? Not likely!'

'I didn't say you were,' protested Sinet rather wearily. 'Try putting yourself in my shoes for a minute, lad. We've been hunting high and low for those hundred million francs, and there they were, on my beat, here in Louvigny-Triage! It's enough to drive a man mad!'

'A hundred million!' Lamy was saying, as though he could still hardly believe it. Then, heaving a sack on to his shoulder, he repeated in the same tone: '*The* hundred million, from the Paris–Ventimiglia express.'

Little Bonbon was picking up the notes one by one, turning them over carefully to examine the front and back and then letting them drop into the sack. He looked up boldly at the Inspector.

'Couldn't we keep one or two?' he asked at last with quite devastating innocence. 'They wouldn't miss them in all this lot.'

The Inspector stuttered with rage.

'If there's a single one missing,' he bellowed, 'I'll have the whole lot of you behind bars, you crew of pirates!'

The ten bowed down before the blast, the girls tittered behind their hands. But Bonbon burst into tears before the loud-voiced Inspector. Sinet was rather ashamed of his roughness, and tried to put things right.

'They'll give you each one or two,' he said, more quietly. 'Probably more; I really don't know. Anyway, the bank's got to count them all up again. They're bound to give a big reward, and you should get your share; it's the usual thing. But you'll have to wait.'

A frightened policeman dashed into the little room.

'Come and look after your dogs,' he called to Marion, they're getting out of hand.'

Marion found her sixty hounds scattered through the building venting their rage on the tattered contents of the Billette Factory. It was a fine sight. The dogs were running madly round, plunging furiously into the middle of piles of decorations and emerging with paper frills round their necks or long beards in their jaws. Some were fighting over a cardboard crocodile and others were acting in a way that was enough to give anyone a heart attack. All this was going on in such an atmosphere of snarls and growls that it made the factory sound like a zoo.

'That's nothing,' laughed Marion; they're just stretching their legs. I'll quieten them down.'

She gave a whistle and soon brought them to heel. Meanwhile Sinet came out of the store-room with the children. He carried the last sack.

'That's that,' he said to Lamy with some satisfaction. 'But we'd better come back tomorrow for a final check-up. Now let's deal with this trash.'

He pointed to the five gangsters lying huddled up at one end of the workshop, handcuffed and guarded by the Sergeant and his men. Tassart led the way and Sinet and Lamy took a good look at them as, one by one, they passed in front of them.

'The fox and the bulldog!' said Sinet, astonished, as he saw Pépé and Ugly pass him. 'The Fabert kid was dead right, and Ugly's no beauty either!'

Gaby and the gang were watching, a little to one side. As Ugly was going out, pushed through the door by a policeman, he turned slightly and hurled a vile insult over his shoulder at the children. Fernand charged at him, his head lowered, knocked him to the ground, and began to pummel his face with both fists, crying at the top of his voice:

'Where's the horse? Where's the horse? Where's the horse?'

Sinet and the others needed all their strength to pull him away, and even then he went on repeating his question with a tremor in his voice. The Inspector turned pale. This sudden anger deeply moved him; it showed him a side of the case which he had tended to neglect in his investigation.

'You mustn't get so worked up,' he said gently. 'We'll find your horse.'

'You've said so before,' sobbed Fernand, 'and we're still waiting. But without the horse we wouldn't have been here tonight and you'd still be looking for your millions!'

'How so?' asked Sinet, astonished.

'The key was in the horse,' Fernand proclaimed. 'Those others knew that; that's why they stole the horse. But they didn't find a thing.'

'No?' said Sinet, getting more and more interested.

'No!' repeated Fernand. 'Dad and I had emptied the

horse out a few days before, and Dad put the key aside without thinking. Then one day the gang and I decided that it must open some door . . .'

'That's all very well,' said Sinet, 'but you still had to guess which one it was.'

'Couldn't have been easier,' Fernard went on; 'the address was on the key.'

'Better and better!' cried Sinet. In a few seconds the whole case had become crystal-clear to him. 'But how did the key come to be inside your horse?'

'That,' said Fernand with a sniff, 'we shall never know. But perhaps you've got some ideas about it?'

Sinet brushed his hand across his forehead and looked up. The only time he had seen the wretched horse had been . . . but no, he'd had enough for one night.

The last of the crooks to go out was Roublot. He had a hang-dog look about him and there was no more swagger in him. Head bent, he passed before the mocking gaze of the children.

'That one ought to have stuck to selling mincing-machines,' said the pitiless Mélie.

All at once their gaiety returned. A funny sort of lop-sided grin appeared on Sinet's face.

'I'm taking you along to the station,' he said to the children. 'We shan't be long. I want you to tell Monsieur Blanchon the whole story, and then you can all go home.'

'I hope no one's going to grill us,' said Gaby aggressively. 'We've done no harm. We just had a bit of fun in our own way, that's all!'

'Nobody has anything against you,' the Inspector assured him.

'And what about my dogs?' asked Marion. 'Do you want me to bring them with me?'

Inspector Sinet took a good look at her. She was an odd

sort of girl, not yet twelve and of poor parents, and yet there was something about her that made you think twice. She was worth having on your side.

'Send them home,' he said gently. 'You seem to understand them.'

Marion laughed.

'I'll keep Fifi,' she said; 'he won't take up much room.'

'Good; keep Fifi, then.'

Marion was the last out, patting the dogs, who jumped wildly up and down and tried to get as close to her as they

could. In silence she led them along the alley until they came to where the Clos Pecqueux lay pitch black before them.

'Away!' she cried, clapping her hands. 'Whisht-whisht-whisht!'

The policemen were dumbfounded to see the pack bound silently off and vanish into the darkness.

CHAPTER 8

The Sixth Man

THERE were no unpleasant consequences for the children, just a few upheavals in their daily round. First of all came three trips to Paris to answer the questions of the Examining Magistrate who was in charge of the case, and they were quite good fun. Of course Inspector Sinet was told to escort them to the Police Headquarters, and it was not the sort of job he liked in the very least. Despite his bottle-green trench coat, his battered hat, and his horse-face, he looked like a schoolmaster on an outing with his prize pupils. When his colleagues ran into him in the corridors they just stood and laughed. Each time they went the children put on their Sunday best, but children's fashions in Louvigny-Triage are not those of Paris, and Sinet got furious when he thought what a sight he looked with the ten children, dressed up to the nines, trotting after him.

The Examining Magistrate asked some odd questions about events which had no bearing at all on the case of the horse. Fernand, Gaby and Zidore brought him back to the subject again and again, but their obstinancy only got the magistrate in more and more of a tangle, and hence in a worse and worse temper.

'I don't want to hear that wretched horse mentioned again!' he bellowed, thumping his desk. 'Only one thing interests me – who is the sixth man? We've five of the gangsters under lock and key, but there's another one still at large. Now, you may well have seen him.'

'There were five in the factory the night of the showdown,' Gaby boldly assured him. Then, counting on the fingers of his right hand, he went on: 'Roublot, Pépé, Ugly, and then the two in overcoats – that's the lot.'

'If my dogs had eaten the sixth man up, there'd be bound to have been some scraps,' added Marion, with an angelic smile.

The little ones sat in a row on a settee. They were rocking with laughter, and even the Clerk of the Court was hard put to it to stifle his chuckles. He got quite red in the face as he bent over his typewriter.

'Now think hard,' the magistrate went on, trying manfully to keep his temper. 'You've told me that for some time before the night of their arrest these men had been watching you. You saw three of them at close quarters on several occasions, and so you were able to recognize them without any difficulty; that's very good! Better still, you finally recognized the two men in overcoats, or so you told me, as the two men who were often in the back room

of the Café Parisien. Fine – three and two make five. But we're still one short, and that's the one I'm so interested in at the moment. The sixth man *must* have been keeping a close watch on you for the same reason as the others. Now, did you see him? Yes or no?'

The children shook their heads and stared at him wide-eyed. Little Bonbon alone put up a confident hand.

'Yes, I saw him!' he announced in a convincingly serious voice.

It seemed as though a great weight had been taken off the magistrate's mind. His outstretched arm cut short the protests of the older children and gave the little fellow a chance to speak. There could be no doubt now that those innocent lips were going to make a startling revelation!

'And who was it, my little man?' he asked Bonbon, trying to make himself sound like a kind-hearted uncle.

'Him!' was the reply. 'You couldn't move an inch without having him on your heels!'

His finger pointed accusingly at Inspector Sinet, who was sitting at the other end of the room, a bored expression on his face. The office dissolved in a gale of laughter. The Clerk of the Court nearly split his sides. The elderly typist and the police officers seated round the magistrate were bent double at the sight of the appalled look on Sinet's face. The wretched man seemed to shrink up in his chair, and he cursed the day the ten children from the rue des Petits-Pauvres had crossed the threshold of the police-station in Louvigny-Triage.

The Examining Magistrate jumped up behind his desk and fixed the Inspector with a terrible glare.

'Well then!' he said suspiciously, 'why were you keeping watch on these children?'

Raising his arm in desperation to the ceiling, 'Your Honour,' Sinet cried, 'it was all because of the horse!'

There was no getting away from the horse, after all.

The Clerk of the Court, the typist, the policemen, and the children went into fresh fits of laughter. The magistrate was speechless: it had got beyond him. He rang for the usher and cleared the office.

'Do you want me to bring them back tomorrow?' Sinet asked him timidly, gathering the children round him like a mother hen.

'Never!' shouted the exasperated magistrate. 'Get out! And don't let me see any of you again!'

Once they were outside, Sinet felt all his anger melt away, and he generously stood them all a cup of coffee and a piping hot croissant. Then the whole gang went gaily home to Louvigny on the six o'clock train.

Gaby was the one who had proposed it, and when it had been carried unanimously, the ten had decided to forgo their next week's *polonais*. As a result, that evening Marion was able to slip a packet of five fat, gold-banded cigars into the Inspector's hand.

'That's to go on with until the reward comes along,' she said, smiling to cover her embarrassment.

The poor man was quite shattered by it all. The ten were lined up on the steps of the station watching him with a look of firm friendship in their eyes, and with a happy air of partners in crime about them that made him feel a good many years younger.

Inspector Sinet never laughed. But now he began to guffaw when he remembered all the silly things that had happened in the last three days. 'Oh, the magistrate,' he spluttered, 'the magistrate!'

The others shared his laughter, Marion more than any of them. She remembered the permanent air of disapproval on the magistrate's face that made him look like a discontented camel. Inspector Sinet held his sides. Nothing was worth worrying about now; he didn't give a brass farthing for the hundred million francs from the Paris–Ventimiglia express. The one thing in life was to join in the laughter of these ten children.

'The magistrate would have had a fit if he'd seen this,' said Fernand, unwrapping the parcel he had been nursing for the last three days. 'I was just waiting for a chance to shove the horse's head under his nose.'

And he showed it to them as though it were some precious relic. Inspector Sinet hooted with mirth, and the children echoed his laughter.

It was a cold and slightly foggy night, but the lights of the Thursday Market shone across the Square. In a flash the Inspector found himself back in exactly the same setting and at exactly the same time as a fortnight before. The market people were starting to pack up, but there was still quite a crowd moving round the stalls. The rosy lights from the Café Parisien gleamed through the leafless branches of the trees. Nothing had altered, except for the rather frightening horse's head that Fernand held, and it seemed to be watching him with a nasty look in its eye.

Gently Sinet pushed the children aside and then walked a few steps towards the square with them. As they came up, Gaby, Fernand, and Marion pointed towards the empty space where Roublot used to have his pitch.

'I was standing there,' said Sinet in a far-away voice, 'behind the fishmonger's stall. The other fellow passed quite close by me in the light of the café. He seemed to be looking for someone. Then suddenly he spotted me and he turned sharp round on the pavement and tried to look as though nothing was the matter.'

'Roublot saw you too,' said Marion. 'He was pretty scared. That's what struck all of us.'

'You followed the man,' added Gaby. 'I saw you both pass between the stalls. When the man walked faster, so did you.'

Round-eyed, the children from the rue des Petits-Pauvres watched Inspector Sinet, and they all seemed to be trying to help his painstaking reconstruction of the events of a fortnight before.

'One behind the other we came out on to the grass in the little square,' said Sinet, taking up the story and half-turning to show them the spot. 'And then he was off. He ran like a stag, head down, and then *wham*! As he turned the corner he went crashing down flat on his face on top of that horse of yours, that you'd leant up against the garden wall. I jumped on him as hard as I could and got out my handcuffs.'

'So there were three of you on the ground,' said Marion – 'you, the man, and the horse, the headless horse!'

'Yes, the headless horse,' said Sinet, looking round him like someone who has just woken up. 'The man struggled like a devil – I even got a good smack in the eye in the fight. Then at last I managed to get the handcuffs on him and I blew my whistle. Almost at once Tassart arrived with his two men.'

'We didn't hear your whistle,' said Fernand; 'the square was too noisy for that. All the same, we saw at once that Roublot had left his stall in a hurry. Where was he?'

Inspector Sinet scratched the back of his neck. 'Well, there was no one at the corner of the rue des Petits-Pauvres,' he answered. 'At any rate, I didn't see anyone when I picked myself up. But you're dead right, lad! Roublot couldn't have been far away. You've got to admit it, someone must have seen all three of us on the ground – the man, the horse, and me. If they hadn't, the hundred million francs from the Paris–Ventimiglia express would still be in the Billette Factory. There was only one man who knew where the money was hidden. Just one man, and he was the man I arrested that evening, that crook from Petit-Louvigny who'd been wanted for the last two months on another charge.'

'Then he's the sixth man!' cried Marion, her eyes on Sinet.

'Yes!' said Sinet. 'He's the sixth man all right, a man called Mallart.'

'Where is he?' all ten children asked.

The Inspector roared with laughter. 'He's been in jail for the last fortnight!'

Seconds later he was tearing round the corner of the

Grand'rue making for the police-station as hard as he could go. The children were left standing on the pavement, rather put out by his sudden departure.

'Well, I don't understand a thing!' said Mélie, looking up at the older children.

'There's nothing more to understand,' replied Gaby, laughing at her. 'It's clear as daylight now. The sixth man put the key in the horse – the key that was worth a hundred million francs.'

'But why did he put it there?' insisted Mélie.

'He'd no choice,' said Fernand. 'With the Inspector clinging to him like a limpet, all he wanted was to get rid of the key, which stood for the hundred million. He saw the horse with the black hole in its neck, lying beside him; he shoved the key down the hole, and there's the end to it. It was only after that that things got a bit hot for us.'

*

Then came the reporters. The case had made a tremendous stir throughout the country and you couldn't open a daily paper without reading the name *Louvigny* in great black headlines across the front page.

'There's no getting away from it,' Gaby told his friends. 'A hundred million francs! Just think of it! That really hits you in the eye! People would do anything to see what a pile of dough that size looks like: ten thousand ten-thousand-franc notes, stacked one on top of the other. Well, we've seen a hundred million. So what? There wasn't anything wonderful about that; certainly nothing to go crazy about. As for the horse – crikey, they don't give it another thought. They couldn't care less about an old carcass without a head or tail to it! So there we are, left in the lurch again!'

The photographers never seemed to get tired of patrolling the rue des Petits-Pauvres, the Ponceau road, or the rue de la Vache Noire, on the look-out for a sensational picture. Ten or twelve times a day a bunch of loud-mouthed, self-confident reporters would burst into their homes or catch the children on their way back from school and do their best to worm a story out of them.

And this was what happened the day that the team from *France-Midi* – twelve men all told, including two crime reporters – tried to drag a really sensational piece of news out of the unsuspecting children, something that would send the circulation of the paper up to the heights of the past few days. But without being told, big and little alike realized instinctively that a trap was being set for them. The editor of the paper thought that the hundred million francs was too big a job for the six who were now under lock and key. It was a big enough pie for others to have had a finger in, and he wanted to find out who those others were.

That was why these gentlemen asked the children the most searching questions on the exact lay-out of the workshops in the Billette Factory; how the mail-sacks were stacked; how thick the bundles were, and how the final clearing up had been done. But the children returned the silliest answers to all their questions; they were not taken in by the show of kindness and their false smiles.

The reporters were rather put out and looked questioningly at each other.

'That's that!' said one of them. 'They won't help us!'

'That's just what we'd like to do!' protested Gaby. 'But why beat about the bush? If you've a question on the tip of your tongue, don't worry, just ask away.'

The reporter turned round sharply. He hoped to catch out the weakest of them.

'How much did you take?' he asked Bonbon drily.

Bonbon never said a word. He looked up at the man unblinkingly, plunged his hands into his pockets, and then slowly drew them out, holding the seam of each between his thumb and forefinger. Out on the pavement fell a marble, a false nose, and a dirty handkerchief: a dusty toffee stuck to his left-hand pocket. That was all. Bonbon pursed his lips and blew a raspberry at him.

'And you?'

Tatave, in his turn, emptied his pockets, letting fall an old coin with a hole in it, the stub of a pencil, and an empty packet of chewing-gum.

Zidore frowned and roughly pulled his pockets, sending out a hellish cloud of black dust, nothing more.

'And the tall one over there?'

Gaby made the pleasure last, like Bonbon. Very gently he pulled out the lining of his pockets and cheekily scattered his treasures on the pavement: ten yards of string, three fine potatoes he was keeping for the 'club', and a banger which didn't go off.

Juan was not in the least ashamed to turn out his two pockets, with holes in both of them, one twice as large as the other. The reporter stuck to it, although he had lost a bit of his confidence. It was now Marion's turn. She was the gang's treasurer and she generally had a few francs on her. But today there was nothing left – all the money had been spent on Inspector Sinet's cigars. Slowly she emptied the pockets in her coat. Out fell two cubes of sugar and a hard bit of stale bread. Fifi was there, and he pounced on the sugar. Marion looked down and smiled as the little yellow dog crunched it up.

Fernand was in his Sunday best, and when he pulled his pockets out they were starched so stiff and white that they stuck out like a couple of fins. Berthe and Mélie had no pockets, so they contented themselves with sticking out their tongues and squinting down their noses. Criquet Lariqué was at the end of the row, and he rolled the whites of his eyes as much as to say, 'I've got a couple of million; it's an awful nuisance.' But it was all put on. He had no more pockets than Berthe or Mélie. His mother had stitched them up to make his trousers last longer. All the same, he had to do something to prove his innocence, and in fact he did better than all the rest put together. Turning on his heels, he bent down, pulled up his sweater in both hands, and stuck out his thin little behind at the Gentlemen of the Press.

'While you're here, why don't you take a photograph?' Gaby called mockingly to them. 'My friends won't move!'

The reporters didn't dare.

'Don't take it the wrong way,' said the oldest of them. 'We're only doing our job.'

'I know,' said Gaby. 'But you shouldn't have gone to all that trouble – haven't you heard the latest news?'

'No.'

'It was on the wireless half an hour ago. Terrific! The Examining Magistrate had the money checked before the officials from the bank.'

'So what?'

'Three different teams of cashiers took it in turn to count the money, and they all made it the same – a hundred million.'

'What? A hundred million exactly?' said the reporters incredulously.

'No,' continued Gaby. 'That's the funniest thing of the lot: a hundred million francs and one sou!'

'That was me; I put the sou in – just for a joke,' cried

Tatave, beaming all over his face. 'And they counted it. It was a present from me: I'm not stingy!'

In one movement the children pushed their pockets back. The exasperated journalists left in a great hurry and in a very bad temper. It was just like the Thursday morning when the children had driven Roublot out of the market. Gaby's banger went off at their heels.

They thought they would have a little peace and quiet after that. But next day the reporters were back in even greater numbers, asking even more questions. Fortunately one of them had a bright idea.

'What we need,' he told the children, 'is a photograph of your gang in the middle of the Clos with all your dogs around you. Do you think you could do that?'

'Not half!' answered Marion, who had been waiting for the chance for days.

An enthusiastic crowd of reporters and photographers gathered in the middle of the Clos Pecqueux. The children scrambled up on to the rusty sides of the Black Cow. Marion whistled.

In the next two minutes, dogs arrived from every point of the compass. It was broad daylight, and all the dogs in the town were out, so there must have been a good hundred of them in all. With a joyous bound they were on the picture-hunters and gave them a grand send-off along the main road. From that day, not one newspaperman ever set foot in Louvigny-Triage.

CHAPTER 9

The Horse with a Head

IT was not until mid-January that the gang was able to meet again in the 'club'. For two days it had been bitterly cold, and so, not knowing what to do with themselves out of doors, they were all the more glad to be back in the dark shed of the saw-mill, now lit by their crackling fire.

'Go a bit easy,' said Gaby, trying to restrain the enthusiasm of his eager stokers, 'or the old girl won't tell Sinet first; she'll send the Fire Brigade straight here.'

Things were well organized. Twenty carefully chosen potatoes were cooking in the ashes, and with an enormous wooden spoon the girls were taking turns to stir the saucepan, in which there bubbled a chocolate drink they had all made tremendous sacrifices to provide.

'It's not very milky, but it should taste good,' said Marion as she sniffed the dark brew.

Feeling that there was no longer anyone to fear, she had left Butor and Fanfan at home in Louvigny-Cambrouse. Fifi alone was there to guard the place, but he had too much to do hunting the rats and mice in the neighbourhood to take his duties seriously. None the less, the children got rather a shock to see a tall, dark figure loom suddenly into the ring of firelight.

Inspector Sinet, hands thrust deep into the pockets of his bottle-green trench coat and his hat pulled down over his eyes, approached the fire.

'I've come to tell you a gangster story,' he said crustily. 'The crooks have spilt it at last, and now we know the whole truth.'

'Really?' said Gaby. 'At last you know how the hundred million francs came to be in the Billette Factory?'

'Yes, we've found all that out and a lot else besides,' answered Sinet, taking a quick look at the saucepan of chocolate.

Little Bonbon willingly gave up his seat and pushed himself up against Criquet Lariqué. The Inspector sat down in the circle of ten with a sigh of satisfaction. He unbuttoned his coat and stretched his frozen hands towards the fire.

'You've got a good spot here,' he said as he looked round.

'We were just going to try some of our special chocolate,' said Marion with a smile. 'Would you like a cup?'

'Well, I won't say no,' answered Sinet. 'You wouldn't turn a dog out in weather like this!'

Marion took care to fill the tin mugs equally, and Berthe and Mélie passed them round. Sinet took his and soon had his nose in it.

'You couldn't get a better cup of chocolate at Macherel's bakery,' he said, smacking his lips.

'There's a bit of everything in the pot,' Marion admitted, 'even a bar of Nutty Nugget. The dregs should be better still. The taste of smoke isn't as bad as all that either.'

Sinet sipped his drink very slowly. The children were his friends and they watched and waited for his gangster story.

'There were six of them in the plot,' the Inspector began at last, 'the bravest four to do the hard work, and the other two to collect the loot. You can't get a thing like that under way in a day or two, and the first four were eight months travelling between Paris and Ventimiglia at all hours of the day and night before they hit on a way of getting into the mail-van without causing too much fuss. Once they'd fixed that, there was still a tricky business to arrange. How were they to make their get-away? You don't carry a hundred million francs' worth of notes in a leather wallet! The crooks then agreed that the best thing to do was to get rid of the loot somewhere along the line, but they thought it was a pretty risky business to hurl the mail-sacks out into the open country from an express going at full steam. That's where this fellow Mallart came in. Of course he knew that trains can only take the Louvigny-Triage at reduced speed, and he knew also that the embankment overlooked the lonely Ponceau road, where he could act in perfect safety after dark. So this was their plan of campaign:

'1. Seize the mail van when the express left Dijon, the last stop before Paris, and quietly chloroform the guards, following the methods of the estimable Monsieur Schiapa, head of the gang, and quite an expert in that sort of thing.

'2. Deliver the sacks at Louvigny-Triage, where Mallart would collect them and stow them away in a little house in the Faubourg-Bacchus, rented for that purpose.

'3. At dawn, Roublot, with his van, was to take delivery of the sacks and leave with Mallart. Both of them would meet the other four crooks on the other side of Paris in a lonely house in Pierrefitte, chosen as a rendezvous point, and there the gang would meet to split the booty.

'Well, then, there was the whole gang about four weeks ago, all ready and waiting for the word from Schiapa, who was getting very useful information about the value of the money consignments on this line. Roublot and Mallart were stationed in Louvigny, and they took good care never to be seen together, because of the risks. Then, on the afternoon of Wednesday, December 18th, Mallart got the agreed telegram. "*Mimosa dispatched today by* 164, *stop. Assure safe receipt and rapid distribution, stop. Signed Horticoop. Nice.*" For the past fortnight, Mallart had been watching the railway, and he noted that the 164 reached Louvigny within a few minutes, more or less, of a quarter to midnight. All was well, the time was right.

'But from then on difficulties started cropping up. In fact, on taking a last look round the scene, Mallart found to his annoyance that in the meantime, someone had fenced off the end of the road where he was due to take delivery of the "mimosa". It was only a light fence and it was quite easy to climb over it, but he would be forced to park his van in full view of the little tunnel which was used by odd railwaymen going home off night shift. What was more, he would have to make several trips with the sacks from the end of the road to his van. Mallart, who's as cautious as he is cowardly, said to himself straightaway, "This job's going to take time, and it'd be much better to have two of us on it." So he tried to get in touch with the cheap-jack to ask him to lend a hand. But Roublot was not to be found! He too had had Schiapa's telegram and was lying low until zero hour.

'Time was running short and Mallart was getting really worried. The only thing he could think of to avoid the slightest risk was to dump the loot on the spot in one of the buildings by the Clos Pecqueux. Winter nights are long, and he would have time to get hold of Roublot. The two of them would then return for the sacks some hours later, after taking the necessary precautions. At all events, Mallart scouted round the tool-sheds in the demolition yard, and was able to lay his hands on a bunch of a dozen or so keys to the sheds in César Aravant's yard and the empty factories at the end of the road. There were only too many to choose from. In the end Mallart took the key of the Billette Factory, the most isolated one, and when he paid the premises a visit, he rubbed his hands. It was a marvellous hiding-place. If need be it could be used for quite a while, should they run into trouble.'

'We're with you,' Gaby murmured, entranced.

All the children just hung on the Inspector's words, and listened enraptured as he told them the story in which they too, had played a part. Little Bonbon, however, couldn't understand it all, and kept puzzling to himself why Mallart had got twelve sacks of bank-notes when the telegram said mimosa!

'At a quarter to midnight,' Sinet went on, 'the Paris–Ventimiglia express slowed into the Triage bend. Mallart was at his post, his eyes searching the darkness, still not believing the plan could succeed. He hadn't long to wait; all of a sudden down the embankment tumbled twelve grey sacks which fell into the muddy road right at his feet. That was it! It took him five minutes to get them under cover in the cloakroom of the Billette Factory, where we found them later. Then he went back to the little house in the Faubourg-Bacchus and awaited Roublot, as planned. If he was early, the pair of them would have time to shift the sacks before dawn. The night passed. At six Roublot still hadn't come, and in fact he never did turn up.

'Like Mallart, Roublot too had had his bit of bad luck. When he got home the night before, he had found a police summons. The great coward really got the wind up, and thought at once that all was discovered. But worse was still to come: he dropped all thoughts of meeting Mallart and legged it for Paris to establish an alibi! The next day he went to the police-station at the earliest possible moment. It was all a mistake! He'd only been sent for to renew his street-trader's licence! Roublot could breathe again, and off he went to Louvigny, to find no one in the little house in the Faubourg-Bacchus. You see, since morning, Mallart, now thoroughly worried, had been hunting the town high and low for his accomplice! In the end the cheap-jack decided to set up his stall as usual on the pavement by the station and to sell his wares while he waited to see what would happen next. If Mallart was in the neighbourhood, he would be bound to see him.

'At about four in the afternoon one of the waiters from the Café Parisien came out to tell Roublot he was wanted on the telephone. It was Mallart, speaking from a bar in Petit-Louvigny. He began by reading the Riot Act to his accomplice for letting him down, then passed the real news: the mimosa had arrived, but there was a slight change in the programme. "Where is it?" Roublot asked anxiously. "Safe and sound," answered Mallart. "I'm carrying the key. There's no point in giving you the address over the telephone. Wait for me by the station; I'll be with you in a quarter of an hour."'

'That was when we arrived,' said Fernand. 'Roublot was working like a black trying to sell all his mincers. Actually, he must have been waiting for Mallart.'

'I was waiting for Mallart, too,' went on Sinet, with a laugh. 'Superintendent Blanchon had just told me that he'd been seen in broad daylight in the Grand'rue. We'd a warrant for his arrest on a two-month-old charge, and I went after him.'

'That was the very moment that Roublot saw Mallart come out of the Ponceau road,' said Marion, 'and then he saw you pass by in the light from the Café Parisien. You should have seen the look he gave you!'

Sinet nodded. 'This fellow Mallart's only twenty-two, and he's got a clean pair of heels,' he said softly. 'I should never have caught him. Fortunately your horse was waiting on the street corner and tripped him up beautifully.'

'That horse doesn't like being shoved around,' muttered Zidore, with a knowing air.

There was still a point to clear up.

'It was just as we thought the other day,' continued Sinet. 'Roublot followed us to the corner of the street. He saw Mallart struggling with me and he saw him slide his forearm into the horse's neck. From then on your horse was worth a hundred million francs to those rogues: *it was the only one who knew the right address*. Now we'd got Mallart, he couldn't get in touch with his accomplices.'

The delighted children bounced up and down beside him.

'Very wisely, Roublot slipped away when he saw Tassart and his two men coming. He was waiting for us to go, so that he could get the key back, and we hadn't turned the corner when two of you came up from the Square.'

'Marion and Fernand,' said Gaby, 'and they didn't let him . . .'

'All the same,' cut in Marion, with the whole gang as her witnesses, 'if you hadn't arrested the sixth man then, he and the money would have vanished and no one would have bothered about our horse.'

'Yes,' said Gaby admiringly, 'you did it all.'

The Inspector bent his head, rather embarrassed by this praise. 'You know the rest as well as I do,' he said. 'You were in it. Warned by Roublot, the four from the express came to search for their hundred million on the spot. They had only one clue: the key was in the headless horse that ran down the rue des Petits-Pauvres at a definite time every day. It was an awkward job even for big crooks like them to manage.'

'And did they confess?' Gaby asked.

'Not everything!' answered Sinet. 'The bank-note plot, yes – they're even rather proud of it. But they won't hear a word about the horse. Not one of them has seen or handled it. That horse hangs over them like a guilty conscience. Come to think of it, you could almost say they were scared of it.'

'Why?' asked Fernand in astonishment.

'You see,' Sinet explained with a slight smile, 'strange as it may sound, it really gets those men down to have stolen the horse. They reckon that a petty theft like that will carry a lot of weight with their judges. The robbery of a hundred million francs was worked out in advance, they knew what would come to them for that, but they've not the slightest desire to get an extra five years apiece on account of a tuppenny-ha'penny horse.'

'Then they won't say what they've done with it?' Fernand asked sadly.

Inspector Sinet paused a moment to light his cigar. 'No,' he answered wearily, 'but they must have buried it somewhere, like a dead body, to get their own back on you. For from the day they found that horse in the road, their luck turned against them.'

'Pah! We've still got the reward!' cried Berthe Gédéon gaily.

Their faces glowed in the firelight and they turned towards the Inspector. But Sinet shook his head awkwardly.

'I shouldn't count too much on that, if I were you,' he said with a snort. 'If the bank were the only one involved, they might hand out a million or two quite easily. But in the first place they never promised a reward, and in the second place it seems they can't quite agree with the other six people who are also in the business. I know what goes on in the big-business world. You get those sharks in horn-rimmed spectacles and they drag it on and on and on till you're left with nothing at the finish. You'd much better forget all about it.'

The children didn't seem disappointed. Zidore raked around in the ashes, and presently he lined up twenty potatoes, cooked to a turn, on a sheet of cast iron. Whereupon the million francs they'd hoped for could gather dust in the bank vaults for all they cared.

'When you come to think of it,' said Fernand, smiling bravely, 'it's really all for the best. Our dads would only have kicked up a fuss over that reward. Yesterday mine said to me that it wasn't his way of earning money.'

'He's not far wrong,' said Sinet, carefully blowing his hot potato. 'Anyway, when you weigh it up, you've had a couple of million's worth of fun in the last few days, and at your age that's what really counts.'

Little Bonbon was munching his potato thoughtfully, his gaze lost in the red heart of the fire.

'What's the matter with you?' asked the Inspector in an amused voice.

'There's something I still don't get,' declared the small boy, with his mouth full. 'It's this business about the telegram. You're sure that Mallart really was expecting the hundred million francs?'

'But of course,' the Inspector replied. 'There he was in the sunken road, and down the embankent came the sacks, right at his feet.'

Bonbon sighed. 'That's a pity! It would have been much funnier, if instead of the sacks, Mallart had got twelve boxes of mimosa in the face!'

*

Then came the best half holiday of them all. Monsieur Douin had been on night duty at Le Triage all that week. He would come back from the signal-box at six in the morning, sleep until ten, then get up and potter about the house until dinner-time, when his wife and the silent Fernand came home.

That morning, Monsieur Douin woke with a start at the sound of a violent knock on the door. Hurriedly he slipped on a pair of trousers, and ran downstairs to open the door for his visitor. He nearly fainted. There was the horse standing large as life on its three wheels in the middle of the garden!

Monsieur Douin rubbed his eyes hard and then opened and shut them several times. But the horse didn't vanish in a puff of smoke. It was really there.

'That gave you a bit of a shock, eh?' croaked a voice from one side of him.

Monsieur Douin saw the bushy beard of old Blache sticking round the corner of the wall. The rag-and-bone man came out laughing heartily, pulling his hand-cart piled high with junk behind him.

'I never expected that!' sighed Monsieur Douin, scratching the back of his neck perplexedly. 'Where did you find it?'

'Miles away!' answered old Blache. 'On a rubbish dump in the country, near Montgeron. Luckily my mates an' I go shares in this business. Rag-and-bone men aren't mean, you know! Anyway, one of my pals over there tipped me the word to come and identify the beast. It was our horse all right. I took it back with me last night and brought it round for you this morning, fresh as a daisy. That will cost you a drink or two!'

The two men carried the horse into the kitchen, and inspected it from every angle. Monsieur Douin was pleased to report that it didn't seem to have suffered from its theft.

Fernand had hung the head up on the hat-stand. Monsieur Douin took it down and carefully held it against the neck of the horse while old Blache stood back a bit to judge the effect.

'It definitely looks much better as it was,' he said frowning. 'That is, without the head. But perhaps it's because we're used to seeing it like that.'

'I'll try to stick it back on,' declared Monsieur Douin. 'Anyway, we'll see what the kids say.'

'They'll be pleased,' said old Blache, nodding his head.

'Sure,' agreed Monsieur Douin. 'The horse meant everything to them.'

Then they discussed the whole affair over a bottle of Bercy-Ceinture.

'You remember what I was telling you the other night, how I met that crook Mallart?' said the rag-and-bone man. 'He said the horse was no good to him. Sez he! It got between his legs at just the wrong moment. The treasure-hunt had only started. Then, *wham!* he came a cropper. It'll cost him twenty years inside.'

Monsieur Douin took a drink and wiped his moustache on the back of his sleeve. 'I'm nothing more than an old fool,' he said simply. 'Why, that key was under my nose that very evening. Out it rolled when I cleared the horse of scrap. It didn't even catch my eye. It was as rusty as all the rest, and I didn't bother to read the label. No, I just picked it up and hung it under the meter. You can always use a key. But you know how it is, once you put something away, you go and forget all about it. A good thing young Fernand's got a sharp pair of eyes. He remembered it a few days later. Anyway, he'd got the others to refresh his memory. They're a terrible lot, those kids, eh?'

*

It was one of those warm, sunny days which tell you that, although it is still mid-winter, spring is not far away. With a clean blue sky overhead even the grimiest house-fronts in the rue des Petits-Pauvres seemed brighter. From two o'clock onwards all the members of the gang came running up out of breath, from all parts of the town.

'Is it true the horse is back?' they said, wide-eyed with surprise. 'No one's having us on, are they?'

'The horse is back all right and he looks fine,' Fernand assured them, smiling happily. 'He came back all on his own – at least, that's what my dad says. This morning he opened the door, and the first thing he saw was the horse, standing there large as life in the middle of the garden. I believe him.'

'So do we,' cried the children, quite happy to play their old game once more. 'The horse knew his way home all right.'

Fernand opened the door and showed them their beloved horse. Monsieur Douin was busy sticking on the head with insulating tape, reinforced by a good dollop of glue.

'That'll hold!' he told the children, blinking as the smoke from his cigarette got in his eyes. 'You'd do better to wait a bit till it dries.'

'We can't wait, answered Gaby. 'It's Thursday, the sun's out. Wait? Not likely!'

The children tiptoed in and walked round the horse, hardly daring to breathe.

'Isn't it smashing?' they said at last. 'He looks as though he could bite you, too.'

Fifi got up on his hind legs to sniff the wooden body, and, wagging his rat's tail, beat their legs like a whip.

'He knows it,' said Marion, flushed with pleasure. 'The dog says there's going to be some fun in half-an-hour's time!'

'Not so long as that,' said Monsieur Douin, with an air of satisfaction. 'Just let me touch up the joint and he'll be ready to do sixty miles an hour down the road for you!'

A few minutes later out came the gang in triumph, escorting Fernand and the horse *with* a head. First of all they had a short discussion outside the house to decide the order in which they were to go.

'Let Gaby have the first turn,' suggested Fernand, to make even the most selfish agree.

'Yes! yes! yes!' said all the smaller children. 'He deserves to! He's the chief! Do let him!'

'Right' said Gaby modestly. 'I'd like to. But you won't be the loser by it. *Buckets of blood!* I'll go so fast the ears will blow off my head; Then *wham*, I'll sail over the barbed wire and land on the back of the Black Cow! Just watch if I don't!'

'Give us time to get to the bottom of the road,' Marion said to him. 'We want to be in the front row at the finishing-post.'

'Down the hill, everyone' yelled Zidore.

Away went the gang down the rue des Petits-Pauvres, leaving Gaby ready to go.

The sun shone gaily on the sunken road and on the Clos Pecqueux, which already seemed fresher and greener. The twisted funnel of the Black Cow stood out against the blue sky. It was glorious. They sat down close together on the bank a little to the left of the cross-roads, for no one wanted to be in the path of the horse and rider as they came charging up the slope.

'Ninety-eight, ninety-nine, one hundred – he's off!' announced Zidore.

The children were fidgeting impatiently, the younger one began to shout with excitement, their eyes riveted to the end of the road.

'Gaby's bound to give us a surprise!' cried Tatave.

They all listened. The afternoon breeze carried the sound of a dull rumble which rose between the houses towards them. Gradually it got louder, and then at the cross-roads of the rue Cécile it died right away, only to grow triumphantly louder still at the last curve. They could see nothing yet, but any minute now the monster would come shooting down on them like a bullet, the rattle and roar making its speed seem ten times greater.

'Come on, Gaby!' the girls gave a piercing scream.

'Come on!' shouted the boys, clenching their fists.

And round the corner zoomed Gaby, head right down to the handle-bars.

Then, good heavens – down towards the rue de la Vache Noire hurtled old Zigon's hand-cart, full of bottles, out of control, and dragging the old man with it. He was just coming out of the Ponceau road. They saw him too late.

'Stop!' yelled the children. 'The horse is coming.'

'I can't!' groaned old Zigon breathlessly. 'I won't be able to pull up until the road levels out.'

And the rue de la Vache Noire sloped down steeply to the main road. With glittering eyes the children watched, caught between laughter and fear.

'Gaby will crash,' stuttered Zidore. 'For certain sure he will.'

'He'll put on his brakes,' said Berthe Gédéon. 'He'll have plenty of time when he gets through the bend.'

'Gaby never brakes!' said Juan. 'He'll go right or left, and the old chap will get away with a fright.'

'Ah!' they all cried, and leapt up on the bank.

Round the corner with a terrible din came the horse, while straight across the road went old Zigon with a clatter of bottles. Neither braked and – *wham!* the horse hit the side of the cart like a shell!

'Bull's-eye!' yelled Zidore, throwing his cap in the air.

Gaby sailed over the cart and disappeared into the grass on the Clos. With a dull thud the cart fell on to its side and in an instant its load of bottles was thrown into the gutter. Old Zigon stood stock-still in the middle of the road. The handles had jumped out of his grasp. He was fuming with rage.

'So once wasn't enough!' he shouted, stamping his foot. 'And now you watch me round the corner to run into me, do you! Heavens above! Look at that, you little horrors! Sixty bottles in the gutter Sixty of my good bottles you've smashed, curse you!'

The little ones laughed till they cried.

'Don't get so worked up, Monsieur Zigon,' said Marion. 'You've gained five hundred bottles because of the accident. I'll show you a whole stack of them in the goods-yard. We owe you that much at least!'

Old Zigon wanted to answer back, but Marion's friendly smile made him forget what he had meant to say. Fernand, Zidore, and Tatave rolled on the bank howling with laughter.

'Did you see it?' hiccupped Tatave, half-dead with mirth. 'Gaby didn't brake, not him! He spurted, and *wham!* He crashed! Like a thunder-clap! I bet he did it on purpose.'

Berthe and Mélie, their arms round each other, were shaking like a couple of jellies. Bonbon, scarlet in the face, was thumping Juan on the back.

'Did you ever see anything like it?' cried Fernand. 'If the Paris–Ventimiglia express came down the road at a hundred miles an hour, it wouldn't be a patch on Gaby.'

Farther down, Inspector Sinet had watched it all from Lilac Lane. He laughed till the tears rolled down his cheeks. 'Oh, those kids! Did you ever?'

'Hi, Gaby!' someone called from the road below. 'Where are you?'

Slowly and painfully Gaby got to his feet, climbed over the barbed wire, and slid down the bank. He wasn't laughing now. He was very pale. In the cheerful afternoon sunlight they gathered round him.

'Have you hurt yourself?' Marion asked him gently.

'No, I'm all right,' Gaby answered, in a daze.

He stretched out his arm and pointed to the rue des Petits-Pauvres, the rue de la Vache Noire, the Clos Pecqueux. It was all their little world, ugly enough in all conscience, but the happiness they found there every day transformed it for them.

'It's all over,' he said.

And he burst into tears.

The children drew closer round him, upset by a sorrow they could not understand.

'Nothing's changed,' whispered Marion, putting her arm round his shoulders. 'You've had a terrific smash-up, too true! But that's nothing to make a song and dance about. It could have happened to anyone. Just ask Tatave.'

'It's all over,' sobbed Gaby. 'I'm useless now. Three days ago I was twelve and I didn't tell a soul. For three days I've felt myself getting sillier and sillier. You saw? I can't even ride that wretched horse any more. I'm finished. You'll have to find another chief!'

All the children cried out in protest. Marion squeezed his arm.

'Don't be silly,' she said. 'You're twelve: so what? Sooner or later we'll all be twelve, but that's no reason why we should break away from each other. We'll grow up together, that's all. The gang still sticks together, just look. They won't stop us having fun together in a hurry.'

'The kid's right,' muttered old Zigon at one side. 'The world's all right if you've got good friends.'

Then, through his tears, Gaby saw nine happy faces gleaming in the golden sunshine: Marion, Berthe, Mélie,

Zidore, Fernand, Tatave, Juan, Criquet, and Bonbon. He smiled.

The darky walked round the pram and came back to his friends clasping something to his chest.

'The horse's head's come off again,' he called, dumbfounded, holding it up in his little black hands.

A new fit of laughing seized the children. Then they had a closer look. The horse hadn't suffered much, but the smash had taken the head clean off.

'Well, it's plain he doesn't want a head!' said Gaby, in a tone that brooked no answer.

And with that he booted it as hard as he could, and sent it flying into the grass on the Clos Pecqueux.

Rather shyly Inspector Sinet came up the rue de la Vache Noire. He kept to the side of the road, for he was rather ashamed to be trespassing on their favourite spot, nor did he like to butt in when they were so obviously enjoying themselves. But his appearance upset no one – on the contrary!

'Hi! Inspector!' called Zidore, pointing to the horse with a polite gesture of invitation. 'Don't you sometimes want to have a go?'

Inspector Sinet closed his eyes, put out his arms, and, a look of horror coming over his face, made off up the rue des Petits-Pauvres as hard as he could go.

The Author

Paul Berna was born at Hyères in 1913. He was the youngest son of a large, quarrelsome, noisy family who had a good deal of fun together. He spent his whole childhood in the south of France, and is still very fond of this part of the country, although he has had to leave it for much of the time since he grew up.

He went to school in Toulon and then at Aix, where he was very successful. Beside liking all sorts of books and literature he enjoyed football and swimming. When he left school he did a two-year apprenticeship at a Paris bank, and then had various jobs which did not much appeal to him. He was offered an administrative job in the Post Office after the Second World War.

Although his other work has kept him busy he has always been interested in books for young people, and his own novels show how well he understands children.

The Street Musician, *Flood Warning*, *The Mystery of the Cross-Eyed Man*, *The Secret of the Missing Boat*, and *The Knights of King Midas* are also available in Puffin Books. His science fiction novels, *The Threshold of the Stars* and *Continent in the Sky*, show that he is just as good at creating the atmosphere of an unknown place as of somewhere as familiar as the streets of Paris or a Riviera town in summer.

In 1960 he married Saint-Marcoux, who is well known for her novels for older girls.

If you have enjoyed this book and would like to know about others which we publish, why not join the Puffin Club? You will receive the club magazine, *Puffin Post*, four times a year and a smart badge and membership book. You will also be able to enter all the competitions. Write for an application form to:

The Puffin Club Secretary
Penguin Books Limited
Bath Road
Harmondsworth
Middlesex